Gym Daddy

an age gap romance

k.e. monteith

Also by K.E. Monteith

<u>Standalones</u>
All Grown Up
Third Time's The Charm
One Dropped Key
Quitting My Boss
Gym Daddy

<u>Snowfall Valley Series</u>
Back When We Faked It
Strike to Burn
A Much Kneaded Union
Crushes & Christmas
Snapshot Problems
Dirty Charisma Check
Give Me a Redo

ASIN: B0C1LRCD8Q

Amazon ISBN: 9798393474683

Ingram ISBN: 9798868927249

Cover design by: K.E. Monteith; Image from: Canva

Printed in the United States of America

If you recognize me from the gym, no you don't

Please be aware that this book contains sexually explicit scenes with mild daddy kink exploration that is not suitable for children.

1

Lucas

"Sir, we've got a problem." Rick poked his head into my office, a grimace wrinkling his young face. Great. Just what I needed, another problem.

"What is it this time?" I groaned, trying to massage away the worry lines. My gym had been open for two years now and it was still problem after problem. Things should have evened out by now and frankly, I was getting too old for this shit.

"Jesse called out sick and her Pilates class starts in a couple of minutes." Rick was already sinking out of view, avoiding the question already forming on my lips. But it didn't matter, because I knew the answer. He couldn't cover Pilates because he had a strength training class at the same time. And since Pilates started in literally a couple minutes, there wasn't time to call around to find a replacement. And the only other folks here capable of teaching the class was ... me. And the last time I taught a Pilates class was when the gym first opened.

Fuck.

I shuffled through the bottom drawer of my desk and pulled out a basic Pilates class routine. The instructors might have poked fun at me for having them make sub plans like school teachers, but I was right to have them put in the extra work. It saved us from the negative reviews of a class canceled right before it was scheduled to start.

Now the only problem was if I could remember how to do half of the positions listed in Jesse's plan.

Fuck.

I rushed to the studio, opening the door to roughly a dozen students, all seated on their mats, pilates balls at their sides. They looked at me, brows raised, heads tilted. I knew most of the attendants, either from events or from when I still covered personal training and classes when the gym first opened.

But it was the girl in the back who really caught my attention. Dark hair, sharp blue eyes, and a band shirt that had been cut and tied in the back. I'd never spoken to her, but she'd drawn my eye more times than I'd like to admit, always walking straight past my office and to the studio. I shouldn't be looking, she had to be at least 20 years younger than me and she was a customer. And right now I should be focused on class, not wondering if I could sneak a look at her ass.

Except that was exactly what I was doing.

Fuck, it was going to be a long class.

"Hello everyone, I'm Lucas. Jesse is out sick, so I'll be covering this class tonight."

Mia

That was, without a doubt, the worst Pilates class I've ever taken. And I've taken a class where I was the only attendant and the instructor decided that meant they should sit a foot in front of me and cheer me on after every move.

As was my suspicion of most men, this Lucas dude was only good to look at. Salt and pepper hair, broad shoulders, and a full face of scruff that I was having inappropriate thoughts about because that was the only thing that kept me going through the five-minute plank he had us hold. Five minutes! Jesse only did a minute for a good reason. Planks fucking suck.

And when class was finally done, I was left with unappealing wet spots on my back and under my arms, something that never happened during the normally *low-impact* exercise. Then the man had the gall to ask people's opinions on how class went.

Instead of engaging in conversation and spewing my valid criticism, I went straight out of the studio and to the cubbies just outside the door. The wall was glass, so now I could see, but not hear, the hot Gym Daddy. Just the way God meant.

"You enjoy class, dear?"

I looked up to see Judy, an older woman who somehow came to every class and was always using heavier weights than me. Was I upset that this 80-year-old woman was somehow more fit than my 27-year young ass? No. However, I was insanely jealous. I may have picked this gym because it was an AARP gym and I had the joint issues of a card-carrying member, but I hadn't expected the older gym members to show me up so hard.

"Class was …" I slipped on my Crocs as I tried to come up with a word to describe the experience that didn't come off as rude. Even if the criticism wasn't directed at Judy, I didn't want the sweet old woman to hear my negativity, of which there was a lot. "Challenging."

"Oh, that's for sure. Poor man probably hasn't taught Pilates in years." Judy laughed, the sound soft and sweet. She was exactly the kind of woman I imagined a grandmother should be. Any second now she was going to pull out a snack from her bag and offer me some.

"Judy." We both looked up to Lucas, who'd stepped out of the studio, followed by the few stranglers who headed straight for the locker rooms. Lucas looked at Judy, nodded, then looked at me. I got the feeling he wanted me to introduce myself, but I wasn't exactly inclined to give this daddy-kink romance book cover model my name after his shitty class. For all the classes I've attended at this gym, the instructors always introduced themselves to every individual and asked about any injuries or medical conditions before getting started. Mister Gym Daddy didn't do that. And sure, it's possible he was only asked to cover class right before it started, but that was far from his only strike.

"Lucas, you've met Mia, right? She's my class buddy." God bless Judy for smoothing over the awkward moment. I gave the woman a warm smile before standing and extending my hand to Lucas.

"Nice to meet you." We shook hands and Lucas nodded but didn't immediately let go of my hand. Great. An old man acting just north of creepy. Except it didn't actually feel creepy like it would with any other man, it felt … fine. Typical hot guy privilege, I guess.

Somehow picking up on my vibe, Lucas let go, clearing his throat before asking, "Did you ladies enjoy the class?"

Judy and I exchanged a look and I instantly knew Judy hated the class just as much as I did. She was just much better at hiding it than I was. Because based on the way Lucas pulled back and crossed his arms, I must've made a pretty bad face. Oops.

"Was it really that bad?" he asked, voice closer to the sound of gravel than actual words. Another issue during class. Hard to focus on the actual words when they're said in that sexy, grumbled tone.

Actually, maybe it wasn't that sexy and I was just horny. It had been a while.

"Well, it's been a while since you've taught a class," Judy said, trying to temper the blow. I chose not to say anything.

"Mia?" The man raised an eyebrow, almost like he was daring me to criticize his shitty performance. And there was no way I could hold my tongue after that look. Or the way he said my name like he was seeing how it tasted on his lips.

"Well, correcting people's posture by calling out their shirt color is kinda a shit thing to do." Beside me, Judy stifled a chuckle. Good to know she's cool with a little profanity.

"Excuse me?" Lucas gasped, shoulders dropping. "I didn't have time to ask everyone's names before class."

"Okay, sure, but that doesn't make it *not* a shitty thing to do."

"Proper posture is important for the exercise," Mister Gym Daddy argued and I rolled my eyes.

"I know that. But there was no need to call specific people out. Just saying make sure you're back isn't arching would've gotten the point across just as well."

Lucas was quiet for a moment, jaw tensing like he was chewing over what he wanted to say but couldn't because I was a customer and he could get fired.

"Do you go to a lot of classes here?" Weird follow-up question, but whatever.

"Yeah, I've been to pretty much every class offered." Which was mostly true. There were a couple of classes that were only held during working hours and I couldn't do barre because of my ankle problems, but he didn't need to know that.

"And you've enjoyed those classes?"

"Yeah."

"And personal training?"

"Ew." It was a knee-jerk reaction because I didn't do well with one-on-one training. It made me overly conscious of what I was doing, which made me inevitably lose my balance or count. I used to dance, so group classes were much more my speed. Plus personal training reminded me of PT. So yuck.

Judy, who'd moved to sit on the bench and tie up her shoes, said, "Mia only does classes with me and the girls."

I nodded in confirmation and Lucas looked horrified. Brown eyes so wide I thought they might pop out.

"You *only* do the classes? Not the training or the equipment?"

"I prefer group classes, everything else is boring." I shrugged, trying to pretend that I wasn't feeling judged for my choice of exercise activities. I mean, who was this man to judge me anyway?

"That's a whole half of the gym you're not even using. You're wasting your money."

"The number of classes I take a month is more than worth the membership. And what does it matter to you? I'm sure the owner doesn't mind that I'm only going to classes, they get my money either way."

Lucas tensed in front of me.

Beside me, Judy chuckled. "He is the owner, dear."

Ah, shit. He wouldn't kick me out just because of a few rude comments, right? It'd be a pain in the ass to find a new gym. I really like this one. Even though the owner is turning out to be a bit of a grumpy asshole.

"I care that my customers enjoy the gym. The whole gym." This man was giving off stern 'I'm about to give you a lecture on utilizing the things you spend money on' vibes. And since he was the owner and I wanted to grab dinner on my way home, I should just back down, mumble an apology, and head straight for the door. Except he opened his mouth again to add, "And I certainly don't want anyone to feel like they're not getting their money's worth."

Sexy gym daddies really should just keep their mouths shut.

"I do. Most Pilates studios are like a hundred bucks for four classes a month. I pay the same here for *unlimited* classes. I think you're just undervaluing the classes because you're too busy catering to gym bros that grunt and sweat all around the rest of the gym."

"That's not what we do here," he argued, stepping closer and looking down at me. Must've hit a sore spot. Good, I'll poke it again for good measure.

"Oh really? Then why else do you keep moving around the Pilates and yoga classes in favor of those stupid group trainings? I've had to change my workout schedule almost every month because shit keeps getting rescheduled."

Lucas took a long, controlled breath. He looked between me and Judy before settling his gaze back on me. I could practically see the argument he wanted to make in his eyes fighting against the desire to not make a scene. I was in favor of hashing it out because … I dunno, I was in the mood and got off a little arguing with this older, sexy man. But unfortunately, Mister Gym Daddy did not put me in my place.

"I'm sorry that's been your experience. We'll take that in mind when confirming next month's schedule."

Boring.

"Right, you do that," I mumbled, grabbing the rest of my things from the cubby and ignoring the way his mouth parted as if to say something else. I didn't need to waste time on men that weren't going to fuck me.

Lucas

The next day, I sat in my office, staring at my computer, at the spreadsheet that held gym members' information. I could look up Mia. I could figure out just how young she was and write off any stray thoughts for good.

Except that would be an invasion of privacy.

And also because after having her argue with me for one measly minute, I didn't want to hear that I couldn't have her. I wanted to live in a world where I could fantasize about her just a little bit longer.

I'd known the class had gone horribly. I was short on time and stressed. Of course, it'd be shit. But Mia was the only one who'd said anything. She might've tried to play it off at first, but I could see her face the whole class. She hated having me there, from the second I stepped in. She scrunched her nose when I selected the music. Sucked in her breath when I explained the warm-up. And rolled her eyes any time I called out a form correction. Had Judy not been sitting with her, she might've started yelling the second I stepped out of class. And I deserved it.

Deserved it but still thought about getting her on her knees for the attitude.

Fuck. I needed to burn off some steam. I hadn't been this horny since I was a fucking teenager and got my first girlfriend.

I snatched up a bottle and towel and headed straight for the treadmills. Or at least that was the plan. But I had to pass the hall that led to the locker rooms and studios. And standing in the center of that hall was Mia.

She was seated on one of the waist-high cots trainers used to help with stretches, fiddling with the TheraGun. She switched out the head and twisted her arm around to reach her lower back. Seemingly unsatisfied, she tilted her arm left, then right. Then she grumbled and switched heads again.

"Would you like some help with that?" I should've walked on by, should've gotten someone else to help her, but I couldn't help myself. Mia looked at me over her shoulder, brown waves falling into her face. Her brow furrowed as she looked me up and down, but her eyes still light up with something that I wanted to read as attraction.

"No, thank you." She kept her voice polite, turning before I had a chance to respond. But given that I had become some sort of glutton for her yelling at me, I set my things aside and joined her. She didn't look up as I moved closer and instead focused on snapping the next head in place.

"You're trying to get your lower back, right?" I stepped over to the display and pulled out the one head she hadn't grabbed. "This one's the best for that."

Mia looked at the piece I held out for her, chewing on her lip. I wondered how argumentative she was when she wasn't trying to look polite. Was she thinking of ways to deny my help right now, how she could argue that she knew what she was doing? I didn't get an answer though, because whatever she was contemplating, she pushed it aside to take the piece with a mumbled thanks.

I knew that was my cue to leave. That as soon as she had the head snapped in place and turned on the gun, my duty to her as a customer was done. But I was too damn attracted to her to turn away.

"Don't you have more important things to do than stare at me, Mister Gym Owner?" Mia grumbled, tilting dangerously forward to maneuver the gun down her back. The reappearance of her attitude made me smile.

"I'd say helping my customers is pretty important."

Mia huffed and rolled her eyes, making a shooing motion with her free hand. "Yeah, well you've helped me, so move along."

"You sure about that?" I nodded to her awkward hold on the gun and she shuffled in place.

"I'd do better if you weren't looking," she murmured before she hopped off the cot and turned away from me. She braced one elbow against the cot, the other arm twisting around her back to position the gun. She turned it on and immediately winced.

"Let me help." The words were out of my mouth before I could think better of them. But I didn't like seeing her in pain. I told myself I'd feel the same for any customer, but that was too blatant of a lie for me to stomach. So I told myself this was the last time I'd offer to help her and then I'd take the hint and leave her alone if she said no again.

Mia turned and her eyes met mine. She looked at me for a long moment and I tried not to seem nervous. Still, I crossed my arms, fingers gripping tightly as I awaited her answer.

She took her time looking me over, her eyes dropping down to my waist, maybe lower. I shifted on the balls of my feet. Her eyes lazily came back to meet mine and she smirked.

"All right, fine, let's see what you got Mister Gym Daddy. Why not?" Mia stood upright, shoulders relaxing as she turned off the massage gun and handed it over. As the gun's weight settled in my hand, her words repeated over and over in my head. Mia didn't acknowledge what she said and I questioned whether I actually heard her call me Daddy as she settled down on the cot.

No, I must've misheard her. There's no way she'd say that. I was hearing things. Hearing what I want to hear.

Why the *fuck* did I want to hear that?

I stepped up beside her, fiddling with the button of the gun as I took her in and tried to ground my thoughts back in reality. She was wearing another cropped top, leaving her lower back exposed. My hand hovered over her bare skin for a moment before common sense caught up.

"Can I touch you?" My eyes didn't leave her back, but I heard her turn to look at me. This was crossing a line. I didn't have faith in my voice not to sell me out and it wasn't like she could possibly be attracted –

"Yeah, go for it." She shrugged and settled back down. I waited for some sort of sarcastic comment, something that would keep me from touching her and finding that I wanted to do more. When she didn't say anything, I let my fingers graze across her lower back, watching how she shivered in response. I started rubbing small circles into her back, keeping my touch light and watching her face. She hummed softly until I hit the tightness on her right side. I pressed light circles into her skin, gradually increasing the pressure until the wince faded.

I let my fingers fall away from her skin and moved the gun to my other hand, turning it to the lowest setting. I let my free hand rest on her back, just under her shoulders, and brought the massager down.

Mia jerked when the head first hit her skin and instinctively my other hand held her down. She stilled underneath me and I pulled away. What the fuck was I doing trying to hold this woman down like that? I'd barely had a full conversation with her and I was already so sex obsessed that I pinned her down the second there was a reason to. I needed to get away from her. Get away and give her space. Maybe even check the classes she signed up for so I could save her the awkwardness of having to see me again. The last thing she needs is some old guy sexualizing her when she's trying to work out.

But then she snorted and panic was the last thing on her mind.

"Lucas, you gotta take a lady out to dinner before you hold her down like that," she laughed, her face now buried in her arms, ears red and giggles shaking her body.

"I'm sorry. I didn't mean anything by it. I'll go." I went to set the massage gun down, but Mia grabbed my wrist.

"No worries, I liked it. Keep going. I'll be a good girl for you and stay still this time." She winked before letting go of my arm and resting her head back down.

Blood rushed everywhere. She liked it. She said she'd be a good girl for me. And that wink …

She was one hundred percent fucking with me. She saw what I was thinking and poked fun at it. And worse, I couldn't tell if she was goading me or trying to gently turn down my unintended advances. But she'd told me to keep going …

I kept my free hand off her, pressed the gun to her back, and started it. I made small circles, back and forth, over the tender skin. Eventually, I pressed harder into her skin and she hummed.

I didn't look up at her. I didn't notice that her hair had a red tint in this light. I didn't notice the small smirk that broke out across her face or how she bit her lip to hide it. And I most certainly didn't notice the way her ass jiggled.

"That's good, thank you," Mia murmured. Her words were soft and content. And something about it soothed me, made me feel … right. And I was far too old to be thinking stupid, cheesy shit like that over a goddamn crush.

"Would you mind doing my thighs too?" She wiggled her legs, drawing my eyes to her ass. There was a lilt to her voice, an implication or maybe a challenge. And I didn't do too well with being challenged.

I stepped away from Mia to swap out the gun's head. As I faced the station, I took a second to clear my thoughts. I was imagining her implication because it's what I wanted to hear. I couldn't be interested in a customer, let alone someone so young. And there was no way she was interested in me.

Returning to her side, I got right to work. Because that's what this was, work. She was a customer and while I wasn't her trainer, this was within the purview of my job. So I focused on massaging circles and keeping my free hand balled in my pocket.

"That feels so good," Mia sighed, the sound close enough to a moan that my brain short-circuited. My gaze traveled up to the back of her head, face still buried in her arms, then down to her ass. Then the curve of her ass. My thoughts wandered to where that curve led. I wondered if she could feel the vibrations there. If I'd be able to make her come by just bringing the gun close enough.

"You getting bored down there?" Mia's head popped up as she pushed up on her elbows and looked down at me. I quickly pulled my gaze up to meet hers. The gun buzzed in my hand, no longer pressed against her leg, just floating an inch over her skin.

"No. Why?"

Mia raised an eyebrow. And when I didn't say anything in return, she pushed up to a seated position.

"Whatever. I'll just schedule a massage. Judy said Aaron was good." She kicked her legs over the cot and hopped down. The TheraGun dropped down to my side, still buzzing.

"No." That one word encompassed all my thoughts. The response to her getting someone else to massage her. The response to another man touching her. The response to ending this moment.

"No? Are you saying you wouldn't recommend someone you hired?" She bent down to grab her water bottle that sat by the leg of the cot.

"That's not what I said. He's …" Aaron was fine. He came highly recommended by his previous employer and had no complaints. My problem was that I wanted to have my hands all over Mia, not the flirt that was closer to her in age. "He's booked. I'll make you an appointment with Tracy."

Mia eyed me for a moment before turning away. "I'll schedule an appointment with her then. At the front desk."

Disappointment flooded me like a bucket of ice water dumped on my head. Shortly followed by the feeling that I was being an idiot, standing in the middle of the hallway, watching her leave, TheraGun still buzzing in my hand.

Mia

"Where is your shirt?" The grumbled words were barely audible over my music, but I'd been waiting for them.

"Sorry, what was that?" I asked, pulling on a polite smile as I took one earbud out and lowered the speed of the treadmill. The treadmill that sat just outside Lucas' office.

Was I being a bit of a brat by continually testing his limits? Sure. But watching Lucas fight his desire to put me in my place or fuck me, or whatever it was that was going through his head, was what I called a good time. And since he wasn't cracking, this flirting by annoying him was safe. Nothing was gonna come of it. Just the way I liked my relationships.

"You're not wearing a shirt," he gritted out, changing the question to a statement, likely because in the few days that I've been messing with him since the massage, he's learned to expect an attitude.

"That's correct." I paused, looking around the gym at several shirtless men and a few other women in sports bras, and then turned back to him. "Is that a problem?"

Lucas' jaw worked, several words forming on his lips before falling off before he grumbled one word. "No."

"You sure? I could go completely shirtless like those guys." I pointed over my shoulder to the men in question, grinning as Lucas' nostrils flared. He really was too easy.

"I thought you said you didn't like using the gym floor." Lucas' eyes met mine and he didn't look away. Not even when I stopped the treadmill and got down with a little bounce. Boo.

"Well, since you mentioned it, I thought I'd give it a try. There's this TikToker that makes music playlists for walking on the treadmill. Wanna listen?" I held out the earbud and tried to smile sweetly. He narrowed his eyes at me, taking a long moment before taking the earbud and putting it in. His eyes fell away from mine for a moment until the lyrics hit him at which point his eyes shot to mine, pupils dilated. I still had the other earbud in, so I heard the music right along with him. As Doja Cat proclaimed her delicious taste, Lucas pulled the bud out and thrust it back into my hand.

"Music can be an excellent motivator. Sorry for interrupting." Lucas abruptly turned away and my shoulders sank. This game wasn't any fun if he didn't play with me a little.

I watched as he returned to his office and closed the door behind him. Resigned, I got back on the treadmill. Not because I really wanted to, I fucking hated walking in place, but because I was already here and I might as well finish the playlist.

Except walking was fucking boring and there weren't any classes anytime soon and Lucas had spoiled my fun. Fuck it, I'll just –

The blinds of Lucas' office pulled up and suddenly the grumpy, older man was watching me, eyebrow raised. Before, his door had been open and he probably only got a glimpse of me when I first walked by. Now he had a full show.

I smirked and turned up the speed.

"Could you please put a shirt on? No one wants to see your suffocating boobs," Carrie said as soon as I stepped into our apartment, tossing a hoodie at me.

"I was doing some cardio, can't have my boobs bouncing all over the place." I shrugged, hoping she wouldn't point out the fact that this wasn't my most compressing bra. And she knew it wasn't because I showed said bra off when I finally found something that prevented the jiggle of fat.

Unfortunately, Carrie looked directly at my boobs and wrinkled her brow. "Next you're gonna say Mister Gym Daddy wasn't there."

I rolled my eyes and collapsed beside her on the couch, tossing the hoodie back on her lap.

"And I guess you're gonna say that the men's shoes by the door are yours?" I side-eyed her, watching as pink flared across her face.

"It's not – they're from – I –"

"Gonna stop you there. I don't care if you're fucking our not-landlord." I only mention it because that's the only reason she gives for not dating Ethan. Except he's not even remotely our landlord, he just works in the leasing office. And for one reason or another, she's been coming up with excuses after excuses as to why they can't be together. "And as long as you don't judge me for building up my Gym Daddy spank bank, I won't judge you for whatever it is you're up to."

"But Mia, if you're not going to –"

"Is that the shower I hear? Do you think Ethan'll give us a discount on our water bill if he's the one using it?" I put a finger behind my ear as if I had to strain to hear the running water. Based on how I could clearly hear the shower running, I'd say he left the door cracked. Poor man. He probably was hoping Carrie would join him.

"Fine, I won't talk about your clear daddy or commitment issues that are causing you to flirt and tease a man you have no intention of fucking."

"Now was that really all that hard?" Instead of answering, Carrie rolls her eyes. But there's something off about her attitude. After a little argument like this, she'd normally turn on whatever background show she was bingeing. Instead, she crossed her arms and distinctly didn't look at me.

God, I wish I made enough to live alone.

"Fine, go ahead and say it." Maybe if she just got it out, she'd quit bothering me about it. I mean, why does she care that I'm teasing Lucas just for fun? At least I wasn't bringing some dude to the apartment. And really, it was none –

"Have you been going to barre classes?"

Oh crap, that's not what I was expecting. And quite frankly it was worse. I always put up my gym schedule for the month since classes kept changing, but this month, I just put the gym's printout calendar on the fridge. I figured Carrie wouldn't bother checking the times I went against the calendar, but I guess she did. "I have, but there's nothing for you to –"

"For me to worry about?" Carrie interrupted and I started sinking into the couch cushion. This is why I didn't let people take care of me when I was sick or hurt, they thought it gave them the right to be worried about me all the time. And I hated when people worried over me. It was uncomfortable and unnecessary. I've been taking care of myself for as long as I can remember and when someone else stepped in ... it felt wrong.

But when I was on crutches for nearly two months, Carrie insisted she help. And I couldn't exactly say no in that condition. So she was the one who helped me hobble around the house, get things out of my reach, and install a shower bar. She was owed her worry.

That didn't mean I had to like it though.

"Exactly. I know what I'm doing. I went to plenty of PT to know how to protect my ankle and what not to do. Plus, since I go to an old person's gym, the instructors always list alternatives anyways." When I pause and Carrie still doesn't say anything or soften her narrowed eyes, I continue,

"And I wear my brace during class *and my shoes*. And you know you don't wear shoes during barre, so like, it's fine."

"Your doctor said you couldn't do barre anymore." Carrie kept her voice soft, knowing that if she tried to be the mom friend I'd shut her down.

From the bathroom the water turned off, the sound shortly followed by the click of the door closing.

"Well, I haven't seen Dr. Mora in like a year, so she doesn't know how much I've healed. I'll stop if it starts hurting, I promise."

Carrie hummed but still didn't look at me as she pushed herself off the couch. She walked straight to her bedroom. A few seconds later, a wet-haired Ethan poked his head out of the bathroom. Our eyes met and he waved, lips sucking in. I did my best to put on a friendly smile and pointed toward Carrie's room. Ethan nodded and took his towel-covered ass away.

Poor dude. I wonder if he's tracked her cycle yet, and subsequently mine. If not, he was about to walk into a mess of post-fight emotions mixed with PMS.

Lucas

After nearly two weeks of Mia running around half-naked all across my gym, using machines she claimed to have never bothered with before, and taking extra classes, suddenly she was gone. She hadn't shown up in days, almost a week now. No classes, no walking in just a bra and leggings on the treadmill right in front of my office, nothing. And instead of being relieved that the constant strain of resisting her was gone, I was worried.

There were several reasonable explanations for her sudden absence. She could be on vacation. It's not like you put in time off for your gym. And our recent conversations didn't exactly invite her to share any personal information, it was mostly me criticizing her use of equipment to have a reason to talk to her. There's no way she would've told me if she had plans.

But also, she could be sick.

Or sick of me.

I meandered out of my office and headed toward the front desk. There was a Pilates class in ten minutes and I wanted to see her when she checked in. If she checked in.

I turned the corner to the lobby and suddenly there she was.

Mia was fully dressed today. Dark jeans, a graphic tee, and flannel covered more of her skin than I'd ever seen. She fiddled with her phone for a moment before holding it to the scanner on the front desk, a duffle bag sliding down her shoulder. When she looked up, she smiled at whoever was manning the front desk before her eyes met mine.

"Mia," I said in greeting. Mia's mouth moved to speak but she bit the words back. Then nodded and moved past me.

And fuck, I didn't like the feeling of being ignored by this girl. It made me stupidly follow her as she headed to the locker room.

"I haven't seen you around recently." I kept pace beside her and while she didn't turn to look at me, I could see a small smirk light up her face.

"Aw, did you miss me, Mister Gym Owner? I would've thought you'd be glad to not have to worry about me scandalizing people with my wardrobe or underutilizing my gym membership."

"That's not what I do," I huff, trying to hide the fact that I was worried the whole week for entirely different reasons. "But if you've lost interest in the classes, I'd like to know. For business purposes."

Mia pauses, turning towards me with a scowl. "I may be younger than you, but I'm not a child. I don't just lose interest in things and give up like that."

Without giving me a chance to speak, she resumed her walk to the locker room. Then, just as her hand hit the door, she turned and said, "And most women don't like working out while they're cramping, just FYI."

This fucking woman.

Mia

Carrie got me thinking. This whole flirt and tease and frustrate Lucas thing was getting old fast, especially since there was no release in sight. And god damn did I need a release.

I spent all of Pilates trying to figure out how Lucas would react if I straight up asked him for a one-night stand. Probably outraged that I'd even consider such a thing because he was too old and I was a customer and yada, yada, yada.

So instead of wasting any more mental energy on that, I watched people pass by the studio to see if any men caught my fancy.

They didn't.

So instead of leaving class with a peaceful mind like usual, I was worked up and horny. Fucking fantastic. Maybe I'll run into Lucas on my way out, argue a little, get some ammo for my angry fuck fantasies. Or maybe it'd be better if I could sneak a peek of him working out, ideally without a shirt, those broad shoulders free and –

"I'm sorry."

In front of me was Lucas. Which was surprising, given that he seemed like the kind of man to avoid a woman when she discussed her period. But even more surprising was that he was holding out a smoothie. The pink beverage was blurred by dots of condensation, the drops of water beading on Lucas' fingers. I took the drink, our fingers meeting for the briefest of seconds before Lucas pulled away. But the warmth of his fingers lingered.

His hands would be so warm on my skin if only I could get him to touch me again.

All right, the plan to get him to agree to one night was back. Though calling it a plan was a bit misleading. I didn't have a plan or even the faintest of clue how to phrase the question to get what I want. If Lucas was going to break from a few come ons, he would've already asked me out.

A few of my classmates loitered by the cubbies, obviously watching whatever was going on between me and Lucas. I'm pretty sure no one's caught on to my game of teasing him and I wanted to keep it that way. I didn't know these ladies all that well, but I'm pretty sure they'd either disapprove of the age gap or want us to be a longstanding couple. The thought of either response gave me hives.

I tilted the smoothie towards the front of the gym where a few tables and chairs were set up in the corner. Lucas followed, setting off several hushed whispers. Fortunately, the women weren't bold enough to follow.

"So, you're sorry for ..." I rolled my hand, gesturing for him to fill in the blank. Instead of speaking, he pulled out a chair and nodded for me to sit. And since I had a new game plan that would likely be undone by being obstinate, I sat.

Lucas sat across from me, arms crossed, jaw working. I sipped at my smoothie as I waited, curious to see what exactly he was going to apologize for. Probably just for making me play the period card. It'd be hard to turn that conversation into a request for sex.

"I'm sorry for my behavior. I shouldn't have been bothering you. I'll refrain from doing so going forward." Lucas pushed back against the table, chair screeching against his weight.

"What?" I'm pretty sure smoothie fell out of my mouth the same way the question tumbled out, splashy and unwanted. Lucas, standing behind the chair, raised an eyebrow. He kept eye contact with me but my eyes drifted down to his lips for just a second. It was pretty clear we both wanted each other and he was refusing to acknowledge it.

Fuck that. If he didn't want to play our game anymore, fine. I'll play with someone else. It didn't matter who, I just needed a dick. And I think I said as much as I stood and stormed towards the door.

"What – what about your smoothie?"

I didn't look back, even though I lived for that frustrated tone, because looking back would mean I cared. And I didn't care.

"I don't want your smoothie or your apologies." Shit that sounded like I cared. I was stepping out of the final double door and stopped to turn and face him. Lucas haltered, feet stumbling back as he moved to not crowd me in the small space between doors.

Behind Lucas, through the glass door, I could see someone at the front desk watching us closely. I felt the burn of my own immaturity. Walking out like that was no better than throwing a god damn tantrum. I should've sat there for a moment, let him leave, and then walked off. But instead, I proved I was too young for him, just like he thought.

I shifted on my feet, took a deep breath, and reached out to grab the smoothie. "I'm sorry, that was ungrateful. Thank you. I'll take the smoothie to go."

But as my fingers touched the condensation-covered cup, Lucas pulled it away.

"No. Tell me what it is you want."

Deep breath, take a deep breath and tell him nothing.

"I want us to fuck each other out of our systems."

Fuck. But now that it was out of my mouth, I had to stand by it. It's not like me saying it aloud changed anything. He'd already decided to stop our game, he sure as hell wasn't going to take this anywhere anyways.

Lucas' arm dropped, his face working through a series of emotions I didn't linger on. Now that the smoothie was within my reach, I took it and made a beeline to my car.

It wasn't until I'd opened my car door that I heard him calling for me.

I looked back to see Lucas crossing to me, long strides, his hands fisted at his side, flexing. He looked, and this was likely my horny ass speaking, like he wanted to take me over his lap and punish me.

When he stopped in front of me, I gave him my full attention. Because, fine, I have daddy issues and maybe a bit of a kink and maybe I wanted to show that if he gave me the attention I wanted, I could be a good girl. Whatever get's me fucked.

Lucas took a breath, eyeing me up and down before any words came out. "Can I take you out tonight?"

I jerked back, cringing. I take back my whatever get's me fucked attitude. Dates sucked, especially when it was with a practical stranger you wanted to fuck. So, you know, the only kind of dates I went on.

"That won't be necessary, I'm only interested in fucking you. You can just –" Suddenly Lucas' hands were on my waist and I was being turned and pushed against my car. He stepped closer, filling my space, my air, all my goddamn horny thoughts. When I looked up, he had a deep-set frown or maybe it was more of a grimace. He certainly wasn't happy with me.

"Do *not* talk about me fucking you anymore until you're in my bedroom, understand?" Oh hot damn, I was making him snap. He was grinding his teeth, eyes flickering all over my face as he waited for a response. I nodded, afraid if I said anything he'd come to his senses and move away. "Good. Now, you're the one who said I should buy a girl dinner before holding her down, so either I take you out on a date or we go back to not talking. Your choice."

"Fine, a date before sex then. But I have conditions." Lucas pulled back an inch, leaning down so our eyes were level, hands tightening on my waist. And then, just like I'd done, he simply nodded. "I'm not paying for anything for this date."

"Of course you won't," Lucas grunted, jaw ticking.

I waited for the I'm not like the boys you've been with speech, but when it didn't come, I continued. "Pick up a Plan B pill beforehand too."

Lucas' mouth dropped, eyes widening, then darkening as he put two and two together. I considered making a joke about him picking up Viagra while he was there, but poking fun at his age might unravel this whole thing. And I was so fucking hot for him right now, there was no way in hell I was chancing that.

"All right. Anything else?"

I hummed, considering my options. I left my gym bag in the locker room, so I could ask him to bring me that. But I'd be back for tomorrow's class anyway, so instead ...

"Kiss me. There'd be no point in going out if –"

As I was talking, there was a moment I worried he'd turn me down and I'd have to stick to my guns and we'd stop talking. I mean, we were technically outside his business, though no one could see us, so it would make sense if he said no. But then he cut me off. With the requested kiss.

And maybe I teased this man a little too much because he came in hard. His hands moved from my waist to my jaw, tilting my head so that when our lips met there was no nose bashing or awkward angels. But there was still a force to his actions that caught me off guard and made me gasp. And the second my mouth was open, his tongue swept in to meet mine.

Warm, tingling heat swept through me, urging a kind of eagerness to get into this man's pants I hadn't felt in forever. I slid my hands around his waist, tucking my thumbs under his waistband and tugging him closer. Lucas grunted in response, shifting his feet so he could push into me. His hands dropped from my face to slide up my back, long fingers spread and slid under my bra.

I just needed to touch him more. Feel the heat of his skin on mine. And
—

Lucas pulled away, stepping out of my hold and pulling his hands free.
The sudden cold from my car door, my shirt still bunched up, was sharp
and unpleasant.

"Give me your number."

I looked at Lucas, my brow furrowing. "What?"

"Give me your phone number, and your address, so I can arrange to pick
you up." Lucas pulled his phone out from his pocket, using both hands
as he presumably pulled up his contacts. I dazedly gave him my number,
thinking more about how I wanted his hands back on me and what I could
wear tonight to ensure that happened as soon as possible.

"Good, text me your address when you get a chance. And drive safely."
Lucas leaned in once more, one hand on my waist, and kissed my cheek
before whispering, "I'm looking forward to tonight."

Lucas

I want us to fuck each other out of our systems.

Jesus fucking Christ, I knew this girl was trouble but I hadn't thought she'd just come out and say that.

After she threw her period in my face, I thought that was it. I thought I'd bothered her too much and I needed to accept that. So I got her a smoothie with the plan to hand it over, apologize, then leave.

Except as soon as I got the apology out, as soon as I'd steeled myself to never talk to her again, her face dropped. And she tried to leave, without her damn smoothie or her gym bag or accepting my apology. And my blood was rushing so loudly, I lost my damn head and went after her.

I couldn't help it. Something about seeing Mia disappointed, disappointed with me, made everything burn. And I needed to fix it. Even if fixing it meant doing the one thing I was terrified to do.

Go out with her.

She'd given me an easy out. She just wanted sex, wanted to *fuck*. I could've left work with her right then and gotten it over with, see if everything would return to normal afterwards. But my pride wouldn't let me. If this was going to be a one-night thing, I wasn't going to do some half-measured shit.

So now I was walking up to her apartment, in a new suit, carrying a dress I hoped was her size. And her gym bag, which I had Jessie grab before I left with a poor excuse that Mia had called and scheduled a pick-up outside the gym's hours.

When I texted her that I was here, I received an immediate reply that she'd be down in a minute. The response ticked me off. Just like when she asked me to pay for everything. I don't know if it's a generational difference or if she's just drawing the line, making sure I understood this was just sex, but I didn't like the idea of her undervaluing this date.

So I went up to her apartment and knocked, fully expecting her to tell me to wait outside or go back to my car.

Instead, she opened the door, head cocked to the side like she expected this. "Come on in, Lucas."

Mia turned back into the apartment and I followed, closing the door behind me. I took a second to look around. The entrance opened into a living room, a record player and several shelves of records the first thing you see when you step in. The walls were mostly empty except for a whiteboard calendar. A key in the corner of the board noted Mia's schedule was in blue and someone named Carrie's was in green.

"What's that?" Mia asked, pointing to the bag I held, the one with her dress. I set her gym bag on the floor and handed her the bag. She held the bag open, peering in with one eyebrow raised. "So I'm guessing what I'm wearing won't do for where we're going?"

I hadn't taken a moment to really look at her, but now I saw the dark lace clinging to her body, lined with an almost translucent fabric that showed her skin color but nothing more. My eyes drifted lower to her skirt, white and black plaid that hugged her body just as tightly as the top. The skirt wasn't technically short, but every time Mia so much as shifted, the fabric revealed just the slightest hint of a tattoo on her left thigh. Logic told me I'd see it tonight, that after dinner I'd get to see and enjoy every part of her body. But that didn't stop the urgency I felt to know what marked her body.

"You could've just told me we were going somewhere fancy. I have plenty of nice clothes I never get the chance to wear."

I tore my eyes off the hidden tattoo to meet her eyes. The idea of taking her out so often that she'd wear every item in her closet twice over crossed my mind. But I shook the thought away. This was about getting over our attraction, nothing else would happen. It wouldn't work out even if we both wanted it to.

"You wanted me to pay for everything. Why shouldn't that include your dress?" In truth, I hadn't planned on getting her a dress. But I hadn't been satisfied with the suits I owned and when I was leaving the department store, this dress caught my eye. It was a dark, charcoal grey, like so many of the clothes I'd seen Mia wear, with a low cut that I knew would torture me.

Mia licked her lips, her brow furrowing as she looked down into the bag. I wished I knew her well enough to see what was going through her head. Instead, I just had to wait until she nodded and said, "Fine, I'll change. Have a seat. Unless ..."

"Unless what?"

Mia turned towards a hallway and looked over her shoulder, hitting me with a mischievous smile. "Unless you've changed your mind about dinner and we can just go straight to the bedroom."

My eyes drifted down to that spot on her leg again and I clenched my hands.

What was the point of this stubborn pride? Why couldn't I just fuck her senseless right now? It's what we both wanted. But there was that nagging sense in my gut that I needed to do this right. That because there were so many reasons we shouldn't be doing anything at all, reasons we hadn't even discussed yet, I had to follow the proper steps or everything would fall apart.

"Get changed, Mia," I growled, collapsing onto the coach and crossing my arms. Mia giggled, the sound refreshing compared to her usual taunts, and continued down the hallway.

"It's just us here," she shouted, "so I'll leave the door open if you change your mind."

I huffed, so she knew I heard and disapproved of what she just said. She laughed but the sound quickly quieted. I don't think I'd heard her laugh before today. Probably because the only way I knew how to safely initiate conversation was to limit the topic to the gym. But the sound, no matter how brief, eased my tension.

"How old are you, Mia?" It was a question I should've asked before I even came over here, but now was the only time I could stomach the answer.

"Twenty-seven. So, you know, my frontal lobe is fully developed and what-not." Twenty-one years younger than me. I was drinking when she was born, graduating college. I didn't know what was worse, the years between us or the fact that I didn't care about them. "How about you, Lucas?"

"Forty-eight."

"And does that age difference bother you?" She'd shouted the words, but they were quieter in comparison to her other question. Like she was nervous to hear the answer.

"Not as much as it should," I said after a deep breath.

"Good, it shouldn't. I'm a grown adult, you're a grown adult, and we met *as adults*. There's nothing to be bothered about here. Age gaps only matter if there's a power imbalance. And since this is just sex, we don't have to worry about generational differences getting in the way of a relationship."

Hearing her say the same reasonings I'd repeated over and over in my head was relieving. But the words sounded practiced, like she said them before. Maybe often. And I didn't like the image that thought created. Of Mia on the arm of a different older man, pulling the same teasing tricks she did with me. Then getting what she wanted and leaving.

My mouth opened to ask the question, to ask if I was just one of many older men she'd been, or will have been, with. But like my hesitancy in asking her age, I kept the words locked up to avoid something I didn't want to hear. So I picked up the first thing I saw on the coffee table to distract myself.

It was a bill from a physical therapist, with a little note scrawled on the top with the payments split up across the next few months. I flipped through the rest of the papers on the table to find the same thing. Different bills from different doctors, none of which were more than a few hundred dollars each, but altogether it was a lot.

Without really thinking, I pulled out my phone and started paying the bills. I didn't consider myself a rich man given that my business was still barely making a profit, but the bills were small enough that I could pay them without a second thought. And after each confirmation went through, I got a small rush of satisfaction.

"What are you doing?" Mia stepped into the hallway and I stood, the papers falling from my hands to the coffee table with a soft thud. The dress fit Mia perfectly, the fabric hugging her, molding to every dip and curve. And just like I knew I would, I regretted the neckline, its sharp dip showing the swell and lift of her breast. She was either wearing some sort of tape or nothing at all.

"You look stunning." I stepped up to her and put a hand on her waist, needing to touch her to convince myself this was real. Heat flashed in her eyes at my touch but she quickly shook it away.

"What were you doing with those papers?" Her voice was stern, sharp, and I had enough sense to be ashamed of myself for looking at something I shouldn't have. Apparently, this woman had the ability to make me feel like a boy in more ways than one. Usually, she just made me feel like a horny teenager, but now I was the kid caught with his hand in the cookie jar. Except the sweet treat was private information about her.

"I paid some of your bills." I tried to shrug it off, but Mia stepped away before I could even complete the motion.

"You shouldn't have done that." She moved to the table, snatching up the papers, her eyes scanning each paper before setting them back down. There wasn't much information to be gathered in the bills, all I knew now was that she had some injury that required imaging and PT But it was more than she'd told me.

"I know." I tried to work out an apology, but the words didn't come. I wasn't sorry for paying the bills. It was so easy to do and it would, presumably, take some weight off her shoulder. I couldn't bring myself to feel bad about that.

"I asked for sex," she said, taking a step back to me, pointing in accusation. "Not a sugar daddy."

I took the hand she'd been pointing with and grabbed her waist with my other hand to pull her close to me. Leaning down, I whispered into her ear, "You called me that before."

"I don't know what you're talking about," she murmured, but the words came out shaky as she shivered in my arms.

"With the TheraGun. You called me Mister Gym Daddy." The word came out through gritted teeth and I gave her only a second to respond. She continued staring at my tie, grinding her bottom lip between her teeth, something I very much wanted to do, especially with her pressed up against my body like this. "Is that what you call me in your head?"

She looked up, stubbornness making her eyes shine. "Yeah, so what?"

I flattened my hand on her lower back and pushed her into me, making sure she felt the effect her calling me Daddy had. Her body eased into my grasp, settling into me. "Is that the game you wanna play? What do I call you then? Baby Girl?"

Mia's face wrinkled and I couldn't help but laugh. "Not that then. How about Princess?"

The wrinkles smoothed, but she laughed like it was a ridiculous suggestion. "I'm not exactly the princess type."

She wasn't. Mia was the kind of woman who was closed off, like she didn't want to be bothered, let alone be worshiped. But …

"Doesn't mean you don't deserve to be treated like one."

Mia's eyes went wide for a brief moment and her breath slowed.

"Then treat me, Daddy."

Mia

It's unfair of Lucas to take me out to such a nice restaurant after thoroughly wetting my panties. In fact, I'd tossed them in the trash of the restaurant bathroom a few minutes ago and was just waiting for the right opportunity to bring it up.

Unfortunately, Lucas wouldn't give me any space to flirt. Every time I tried to graze his leg with my foot, he'd move away and shoot me a stern look. Instead, he asked about my job, my friends, shows and movies I enjoyed recently. It made this feel like a real date instead of just a prelude to sex.

"And how about your family?" Lucas asked as he cut into his steak. I set my fork, twirled full of pasta, down, appetite waning.

I needed to get this back on track. This was supposed to be a fun night where I finally got the man I'd been fantasizing about. Not a night where he asks me one question and I start trauma dumping. And if he was willing to pay random bills he found, what would he do when I laid out my mess for him?

No, that's not what this was about.

"Did you get the pill?" I didn't have to ask to know he had. That was the kind of man Lucas was, he said he'd do it and he did. But I needed him to go back to being sexually frustrated with me. I didn't want a soft conversation or concern about my medical bills. I wanted to be fucked, hard.

"Of course," he said after a deep breath.

"Good. I don't like condoms, there's always too much or too little lube, you know? I'd rather just go bare." Lucas' eyes darkened and though I tried to resist it, I felt my lips twitch into a smirk. He was almost too easy.

"Mia," he warned.

"What? We have to discuss it at some point and I'm hoping that by the time we get to your place, you won't be able to wait anymore." Hopefully, the words came out smoothly and covered the worry they held. I pictured his hands all over me, barely able to open the door. If it wasn't like that, then he didn't want me as much as I did. And I didn't want to take that blow to my ego.

"Well I got the pill, so we don't have anything more to discuss. Now eat and tell me about your family." Lucas' eyes dropped back to his food and I waited until he had a piece in his mouth before speaking.

"I'd rather tell you about how I fantasized about you."

Lucas coughed and quickly moved for his water. As he drank, Lucas eyed me with the kind of intensity that said I was in trouble. The look only egged me on.

"Not anything too extreme, just you pulling me by the straps of my sports bra, kissing the shit out of me before putting me over your knee and –"

"Enough, Mia." His voice was like gravel, low and choppy, like he was barely holding on. That sound fed something inside me.

"I was just –"

Lucas stood and slid out from our booth. He took one step and then he was sitting next to me, gently sliding me in to make room. He reached over the table and grabbed his plate, repositioning our meals so they were in front of us.

"You need to get off that bad, huh?" Lucas braced his left arm behind me on the bench and his right hand grazed up my leg. I looked up to meet his dark gaze and fuck yes. I nodded and then my eyes flashed to our surroundings. It was a dark restaurant with high-backed booths. No one was seated beside us and from where we sat, I couldn't see anyone facing us at the other tables. And if I couldn't see them, they couldn't see me, right?

"As long as you're quiet, Princess, no one will notice. Let me take care of you." His hand splayed out over my leg, sliding up my thigh before gripping and pulling me open. "But know I'm going to punish you for this later. Just like you dreamt about."

The rush of heat hit me with a gasp and Lucas covered the sound with a kiss. Despite the way his hand was gripping me, his kiss was gentle, soft presses to keep me quiet. That is until his hand slid further up and his fingers hit hot, wet skin. The kisses stopped and he growled into my mouth, fingers sliding down to my bare cunt. "Where the *fuck* are your panties?"

His fingers dug into my skin, the tip of his middle finger on the edge of my opening.

"I threw them away, they were dirty."

"Hmm. And who's fault is that?" Lucas bit my lip, a sharp sting that only heated everything further. He pulled his hand up until a finger rested on my clit and started moving in slow circles. "Go on, tell me, Princess. What's got you so worked up that you can't sit through one meal without begging to get fucked?"

"It's your fault," I murmured, struggling to keep still. Lucas' free hand went around my neck and draped over my chest, pushing my back against the booth.

"Is it now? Funny, last I checked, you were the one talking about fantasies." He circled my clit faster and the last of my stubbornness melted away.

"I'm excited," I confessed and he rewarded me by sliding his finger down and inside me. He went slowly, humming as he slid in with ease.

"I'm excited too. But you can't act out like this in public." He pulled out, then pushed two fingers back in. I bit my lip, barely muffling a whimper as he started to stroke my G-spot. I'd worked myself up so much just thinking about having him and now I was gonna cum from the slightest touch. "So when we get home, *after* I've had a chance to fill up this cunt, I'll punish you just like you've been fantasizing about. And then I'll fuck you again for good measure."

Fuck. Despite the heat blazing inside me, his words gave me a full-body shiver. When was the last time a man's *words* sent me into such a tizzy? And when he started stroking faster, pressing his palm against my swollen clit, I couldn't help but whimper. His fingers instantly stilled and the whimper turned into a whine.

I didn't *want* to pout, I fucking hated the concept, but god damn, this fucker had me right on the edge. And there was nothing, absolutely nothing, that I needed more in this moment than to come. Lucas, whose eyes hadn't left mine since he sat beside me, grunted and moved his free arm out from behind me. It wasn't a smooth movement, his elbow pressed into my chest as he reached for something out of view. And all the while, my body pulsed in anticipation, my vision going blurry. Eventually, Lucas' hand came back into view with a fork twirled full of pasta. He held the food to my mouth, gently pressing the prongs to my bottom lip.

"Eat your dinner, Princess." He started rubbing against my G-spot, grinding his palm against my clit, just your run-of-the-mill sexual torture that kept relief at bay. "Eat and Daddy'll make you come."

My mouth fell open and I dutifully took a bite. The pasta was smooth, the sauce rich with garlic. And while this was the nicest place a date has ever taken me, the food paled in comparison to how he touched my body. He kept things quiet, rubbing where there normally would have been thrusting, but the difference made things burn. Before I knew it I was completely melted, my orgasm coming like an uphill climb, once I was over that hump, relief came in a quick rush.

As my breathing slowed, Lucas set the fork down and wrapped his arm around me. I sunk into him, inhaling his musk that my post-orgasm brain couldn't describe but thoroughly enjoyed.

"You think you can behave until we get home now?" Lucas murmured, holding me to his chest and kissing the top of my head. Just as I was about to say yes, he pulled his fingers from me and put them in his mouth. His eyes rolled to the back of his head and a soft grunt parted his lips.

"No." How could I behave when I just saw this man moan from my taste?

"Of course not," he sighed, letting go of me and moving out of the booth. He took my hand and pulled me to the edge. "Go clean up. I'll get dessert to go."

I stood but Lucas didn't move, so I wound up pressed against him. Which was *not* a bad position. And I used the opportunity to feel him up. I don't know what gave me a bigger ego boost, how hard he was or how he leaned towards me like his body was desperate for some relief.

"Stop testing me, Mia. I gave you what you wanted, now do what I say," he ground out, hand wrapping around my wrist and pulling my hand away from him.

I hummed in reply and he let go. I took a moment to readjust my dress, then stepped away. "Whatever you say, Lucas."

Lucas

Whatever you say, Lucas.

It was bullshit. She might've meant it as she sauntered off to the bathroom, but by the time she came back, she suddenly wasn't so eager to get home. She answered all the questions she'd sidestepped before. She ate all her dinner, then had us stay for dessert.

Now that her sexual appetite was sated, for now, Mia happily went on with the date as if nothing happened, as if she hadn't been trying to make this just about sex moments before.

Meanwhile, I was sitting there with an erection so painful, I wasn't sure how I was going to walk out of this damn restaurant. Every time she spoke, my eyes lingered on her lips, wondering how soon I'd be able to feel them against my skin, my cock.

"Back when I was still dancing, my studio was right next to this grilled cheese place, like that was all they sold. And they had like three, five, seven cheese sandwiches, and that seven cheese one was absolute perfection." Mia made the chef's kiss motion and beneath the horror of what such a sandwich could do to my stomach, I caught that small detail, something she'd not mentioned, something that felt buried amongst everything else she'd said.

"You danced?"

Mia froze, fork piercing the last bit of cake, eyes wide. Slowly, she licked her lips, the act thoughtful. She nodded without saying anything more, shoving the last of the dessert in her mouth.

That confirmed it. Dancing and the reason she stopped was something she held close, something she wasn't willing to share with someone she was just fucking. The fact that she was keeping that line drawn, enforced by a brick wall, made me unreasonably angry with her. Even though our age difference meant we'd never work as a couple, even though there'd be judgment that might affect my business, I *wanted* to know her. And the denial burned.

"Are you ready to go?" The words came out shorter than I intended, but I was ready to get her under me. Ready to have her and then stop thinking about her.

"Eager to punish me?" She smiled, the tilt of her lips mischievous, and an idea came to mind.

"Yeah. I am."

Mia rocked on her feet as she waited for me to unlock the door. Her eyes darted around the complex, absorbing every detail. But when the lock clicked open, her focus snapped back to me.

I was careful not to touch her as we left the restaurant. Not when we walked back to the car, side by side. Not during the car ride here. And not when I guided her up to my door. But now, when I was just seconds away from having her to myself, I settled my hand on her lower back and pulled her against me as we stepped inside.

As soon as the door was closed, I scooped her up by the ass and pressed her against the door. Mia's leg wrapped tightly around my ass, the action hiking up her dress and pressing her bare pussy against my cock. It might've been my imagination, but I swore I could feel her heat through my clothes and the sensation drove me wild.

I grabbed her bare thighs pulling her closer, tighter, relishing the warmth of her skin, the smoothness. My hands moved up, up, up, until I was touching where the tattoo I still haven't seen would be. I pressed sloppy kisses to her neck and her head fell back against the door. Soft moans and whimpers fell from her lips, her sounds were louder, unmuffled, and more *filling* than they'd been in the restaurant. And I needed more. *I need so much fucking more.*

Pushing my hips into Mia, I pinned her between me and the door, freeing my hands to tear at her dress. I gripped the neckline and tugged, the seam down the front coming apart with little effort.

"Asshole," Mia whispered, though I imagined it had less bite than she intended. "I was going to keep that."

Keep it. She was going to keep the dress I'd got her for what? To wear out on a date with another man?

I tried to dismiss the thought, tried to forget about the possibility as I held her up by the hips and she moved to let the dress fall off her arms. But when the fabric hit the floor and her arms wrapped around me, the anger that thought provoked had wholly overwhelmed me. I pressed her harder against the door and nibbled at her neck.

"I'll get you another dress, one that doesn't come apart so easily." I thrust into her slowly, letting her feel every inch of frustration. "Or maybe I'll get one that's even easier to rip off."

Mia whined something incoherent and I pulled back from her neck just enough to see her pouting lip. I sucked her lip into my mouth, grazing the soft skin with my teeth before kissing her.

th before kissing her. "Don't pout, you're gonna get everything you want tonight."

10

Mia

Everything in my body was buzzing. For a minute, on the drive to Lucas', I thought that maybe the real thing wouldn't be as exciting as him fingering me in the restaurant. I mean, after that he wouldn't so much as touch my shoulder. But fuck once he finally touched me, everything went ablaze.

"I want you. Now. Please." My words came out ragged and broken. It was hard to get anything out when all I wanted was for him to fuck me right up against this door.

Lucas grunted, hands tightening on my hips as he pulled me to him and stepped away from the door. As he walked, I started kissing up his neck, enjoying how his grip tightened in response. With the positions of our heads, his lips were right against my ear, letting me catch every soft groan my actions inspired.

We turned a corner and suddenly I was dropped down to a bed, bouncing against the soft surface. Lucas moved away, hands going to my legs to unwrap them. Except I was stubborn and didn't want to let go, didn't want to lose the warmth of him or his weight between my legs.

"Mia," he warned and I held tighter, squeezing my thighs and raising my hips so my cunt grazed over his cock. There was already a noticeable dark spot over his bulge. The sight made my mouth water.

Lucas' arm covered my waist and he pushed me down to the bed, forcing my legs to fall from him. He kept his hold on me while he stepped back. "I bought you dinner, now do as I say."

A flash of his face, wide-eyed from my comment about pinning me down, came to mind. He looked so different now. His eyes were completely dark, the brown glint lost in arousal, and he was licking his lips like he was ready to eat me alive if I didn't do whatever it was he wanted.

I let my body relax under his hold and settled my legs over the edge of the bed. He held me down for a moment longer before standing. While undoing his tie, he nudged my legs apart with his knees. "Stay just like that for me."

His eyes roamed over my body, spending long moments on the tattoos of constellations that went from my left thigh to around my hips, stopping just below my ribs. He'd been staring at them when he came to pick me up too, though he couldn't have seen much. My skirt hadn't been *that* short.

Lucas continued to undress as he took me in. As each item of clothing fell to the floor, he stared at a different part of me. For his jacket it was breasts, for his shirt it was the dip of my waist, but for everything else, it was my pussy. And when he'd finally pulled his boxers down, his cock bobbed and a little whimper escaped my mouth.

Lucas finally met my eyes and grinned, the crooked slant of his lips tugging at something inside me. I'd never seen him smile before. The man had a resting grimace and my teasing had only made it worse. But the smile made him look relaxed, like he was having fun with me in this moment.

"You excited for me?" There was a glint in his darkened eyes, a look that I somehow recognized as trouble, that made me shiver.

"Yes," I said, my voice barely above a whisper. Lucas' grin widened. He reached for something at the edge of the bed, but I didn't move my head to look. I was determined to be a good girl and follow his instructions, to the point of malicious compliance.

"Lift your hips."

Pulling my feet to the edge of the bed, I brought my hips up and held the bridge. Lucas slid something firm and plush underneath me and I chanced a glance down. It was one of those made-for-sex pillows, the kind that angled you *just right*. And I hated it.

This wasn't something you could just buy at Target or the mall or whatever. And I knew for certain the closest sex shop didn't have these in stock. And there wasn't enough time to order it for me. Which meant he'd gotten it for someone else.

I kept my hips up, hovering over the pillow. When Lucas noticed, his grin fell. "Put your hips down."

I bit my lip but did as I was told. Sort of. Instead of relaxing into the pillow, I lowered my hips so there was just a breath of space remaining. Lucas had bent over, presumably to get something else, but when he stood and saw I'd barely complied with his orders, he pushed me down with one hand splayed across my stomach.

"Are you being a brat in hopes that I'll spank you before I fuck you?" he asked and I let out a slow breath in relief. I don't know why I cared about the damn pillow. It's not like I believe Lucas hadn't washed it between uses. I just didn't –

Lucas' finger slid into my pussy without warning. I was so wet for him that there was no resistance, but the suddenness of it made me clench. He waited for me to relax, then added another finger, thrusting in and out at a vicious place. Normally I was a clit based orgasm kind of girl, it took a lot of build-up for penetration to feel good. But *fuck*, Lucas had done that work.

"I'm still waiting on an answer." He was still standing over me, one leg between mine, holding me open, the other propped on the bed with his knee. His eyes didn't leave mine, but even under his watchful gaze, I didn't say anything. He was wrong. It wasn't brat-like to not want to use someone else's sex pillow. And while I'd definitely spent many long showers thinking about him leaving my ass red, I was too eager for his cock to skip right to it.

"Fine, don't tell. But we're going to play a little game to see how many times I get to spank you. Okay?"

"Game?" I hadn't expected that. I assumed he'd just spank me until I cried mercy. "What kind of game?"

Lucas' grinned again and my irritation about the pillow eased. Probably because I had something new to focus on and not because of how I felt about his smile.

"You're going to pick a song to sing along to while I fuck you. For each time you stop singing or say the wrong words, you'll get spanked."

11

Lucas

"**N**ow, pick a song." I slowed the pace of my hand finger fucking her and held up my phone with the other hand. Mia closed her eyes, lips pursed.

"Mr. Brightside by The Killers."

I leaned down and kissed her forehead and she shook in response. There was something about seeing her like this, responsive and compliant, that fed me. And I tried not to wonder why or dwell on how much I'd miss it once she was gone while I pulled up the song.

I set the phone next to her head and took my fingers out of her. She whined but quickly quieted when I positioned myself between her legs. I let myself take a moment to look at her. Her hair was frizzy now, splayed across the waterproof blanket I'd laid down before I went to pick her up. Her skin was flushed, her cheeks pink, and there were small red marks where I'd grabbed her. And the *tattoos*. They were lines that connected stars to freckles to make the night sky, covering her left hip and down her thigh. I wanted to trace the constellations over and over again with my tongue until I was sick of it.

Beneath me, Mia squirmed, wrapping her legs around my waist to pull me closer. I chuckled and moved her legs to where I wanted them, on my shoulders. I let my cock rest on her, my shaft sliding up and down her clit. She was so swollen, so ready for me that each pass made her tremble.

I looked up at the music player to confirm the runtime. I had almost four minutes to make her come. Just four minutes to keep myself together before I could fill her up. If how I jacked off to the image of her this morning was any indication, I wasn't sure I'd last that long.

"You ready?" My finger hovered over the play button as my other hand positioned my cock to her entrance. Mia nodded eagerly, leaning up to wrap her arms around my neck and watching where we were about to be joined.

I pressed play and gently slid into her.

We both moaned and relaxed into each other. The beginning instrumental gave Mia a second to relax and get used to my intrusion. And it gave me a moment to take a few deep breaths to keep myself from immediately coming. She was so damn hot and wet, tensing around me erratically. It was hard to focus on breathing let alone postponing my orgasm.

Then Brandon Flowers started singing and I pulled back my hips, waiting for Mia to start singing along. When she didn't, I thrust back into her, catching her gasp with a kiss. "You're racking up spankings, Princess."

Mia mumbled something I couldn't catch and started to sing along. The words came out hoarse and shaky. I nuzzled into her neck, kissing, sucking, licking the sensitive skin beneath her jawline, grinning whenever her voice faltered.

Chasing the joy of getting her to miss words, I pressed a palm to her lower stomach, pushing just enough so she'd feel my weight, feel the change in how my cock pushed inside her. I wasn't even keeping count of her spankings anymore, I just wanted to see her break focus, feel her tense underneath me, and watch her struggle to get her mind back in place. The way her voice wavered, the lyrics coming between gasps and moans. It was beautiful and so *fucking* addicting.

"You're doing amazing, Mia," I whispered into her ear, praying the words portrayed at least half of what I was feeling. There hadn't been a second where I thought Mia wouldn't live up to my imagination. But she was so much more than I'd pictured, warmer, wetter. She was too much. And I needed to wring out everything I could get.

But I was too worked up over this girl and now that I had her under me, I couldn't last. I was pounding into her so hard, mindlessly fucking her without any tact, because I needed her now, needed her to feel me tomorrow, and I simply *couldn't* hold back.

The song had just gotten to the first musical break and already heat twisted inside me, threatening to pour out. I just needed to hold on a little longer. I needed to feel her come around me.

I took my hand off her stomach, licked my thumb, and brought it to her clit. Mia bucked her lips, the word 'cage' going higher. Moving my thumb faster, I kissed up her jawline and up to her lips. Mia struggled to get words out as I nibbled at her bottom lip and her voice faltered into a whine.

"I wanna see you come again, princess. What does Daddy need to do to get you there?"

I adjusted to calling myself Daddy far too quickly for my liking. But when she'd said it a second time, called me a sugar daddy, I realized I wanted more of it. And since this was a one-night thing, there was no time for shame or adjustments.

Plus any embarrassment or second thoughts were quickly washed away by how her pussy pulsed in response. I couldn't help but wonder if she was doing it on purpose, trying to make me come before I was ready. Or maybe it was a matter of pride for her too. In the same way I wanted to see her break focus, she wanted to see me come apart for her. I just needed to convince her to let me have my way first.

"You feel so fucking good, Mia. So good I'm struggling to keep this game up." I kissed her cheeks, her forehead. Each word of praise made Mia's body melt into the bed, hands falling from my neck and down my arms. And it was just another thing I wanted more of. "And you're doing so well.

Listening to your voice quaver is my new favorite sound. But it's no fun if we can't finish the game because you made me come too quickly."

Mia hummed and her hands left my skin. I didn't even know what she was doing, but I didn't like it. I moved one knee up on the bed and used the hand that was braced by her head to grab her wrist and bring her hand back to my chest.

"Hands on me," I growled. "I'm taking care of you, understand?"

Mia huffed out but moved her other hand, which had started pinching her nipple, to my arm. She squeezed my arm, nails digging into my skin when I leaned down to suck the nipple she'd been playing with. She tasted sweet, a hint of coconut teasing my tastebuds. I imagined her getting ready for tonight, slathering on lotion, making sure everywhere I touched was soft and smooth.

I liked the idea of her getting ready for me far too much for this to be a one-night thing.

And I took that frustration out on her. I swirled my tongue roughly over her hardened nipples and sucked. Mia cried out, nails digging into my skin, no longer singing but making delectable little whines as I moved to the other breast to copy the motions.

"Lucas," Mia whimpered my name as she finally came. My name, not Daddy or some other joke, my name.

Her orgasm shook through her body, harder than the one at the restaurant, drawing long moans and whines. I wrapped my arms around her, holding her against my chest and burying my face in her hair as I finally let go. My orgasm wasn't what I'd expected. It wasn't overly explosive or followed by a sense of satisfaction. It was a warm relief. Like my body was sighing *finally*.

I let myself hold her for a moment longer, focusing on the way our breaths moved in tandem, the way our bodies relaxed into each other. The music had shifted to the next song, something too upbeat for this quiet moment. So, after a soft kiss, I pulled away.

"All right, Princess, can you tell me how many spankings you owe?"

12

Mia

"Ummmmm." I held the sound, too dazed and distracted to give Lucas an answer. The man had given me a task while pounding the ever-loving shit out of me and expected me to keep count. No way.

"Mia," Lucas warned. He'd pulled away from me, just enough to create distance, though his hands were still on my waist and my legs still draped over his shoulders. His thumbs were gently stroking my skin and I wondered if he was doing that consciously or not.

"Seven?" I guessed, knowing that was nowhere near close. I'd been relatively confident that when he hit play, I'd be able to sing Mr. Brightside with only a few missed words. Turns out I didn't know the song as well as I thought I did. Or maybe Lucas was just that distracting, not that I'd admit that to him.

"Is that so?" Lucas asked, quirking an eyebrow.

"Yup, just seven." I looked at his brow, not able to look him in the eye as I blatantly lied. Lucas chuckled, leaning back into me and nipping my ear. I jumped and Lucas braced an arm over my waist and pinned me down.

"Is that the answer or your limit?"

"Depends on how strong you are."

Apparently, that answer was a bit too bratty for Lucas' liking because suddenly everything blurred as I was flipped over. Lucas' hands were rough, pulling me up to my knees and pressing my back down. And all I did was try to catch my breath between giggles.

"Lucas, what about the mess?" I giggled, pressing my thighs together to keep anything from dripping onto the sheets.

I wasn't normally giddy after orgasms. I was a wham, bam, thank you, ma'am kinda gal. Except maybe I wasn't. I can't remember the last time I had sex with a dude where I'd come more than once and knew more orgasms were coming. This might just be what it feels like to be well and truly fucked to satisfaction.

"Don't worry about the mess. I wanna see it." Lucas moved off the bed and yanked my knees apart. I angled my head, watching his eyes focus on where his come was sliding down my thighs. His thumbs did that gentle stroke thing again and something about that and his look quieted me.

"But the sheets?" It took a moment, and for a second I thought I'd spoken too quietly, but Lucas finally looked up to me. I would've thought that the hunger in his eyes would die down after he came. But if anything, he looked hungrier. Like he was mad at me for making him like this and he was going to use me until he'd had his fill. That look had a very distinct effect on my insides.

"I put down a blanket," he murmured before his gaze returned to my ass. His hands moved to massage his new obsession, his touch possessive.

"Am I gonna need a safe word?"

Lucas' hands froze on my ass, shifting to that soft stroking again as he met my gaze. "Do you want me to keep going if you say stop?"

"No."

"Good. This isn't a scene or about pushing you past your limits."

"What's it about then?"

Lucas' eyes narrowed and he yanked my legs closer to the edge of the bed.

"It's just like you said. This is about getting each other out of our systems. And for me to do that, I need you to feel at least one percent of the pain you put me through these last few weeks."

His hand came down hard enough that the sound echoed in my ear and I jerked away. One of Lucas' hands took hold of my waist and jerked me back into place. The other hand smoothed my flesh and that's when I really felt the sting. His touch was sharp and so damn hot. It didn't hurt so much as it burned. And fuck it if that sensation didn't make me wetter than I already was.

"Too much?" I didn't have it in me to respond. I mumbled something that got the point across though and Lucas' hand landed on my other cheek.

"Shit," I hissed, clutching at the sheets. He'd put down one of those sex blankets that absorb liquids or whatever. I nudged it away, so I was grabbing *his* sheets, not some stupid blanket that he used with every woman he brought home. If I was fucking him, my scent better damn well be left behind somewhere. Out of his system or not, I wanted him to remember me in his bed and think of me every time he –

Those petty, stupid thoughts were chased off by Lucas biting my ass. Not just a graze of teeth or a nibble, but a full bite. The might leave a mark kind of bite.

"I asked you a question, princess. Whatever you're thinking about, stop it. You're in my bed, keep your focus on me." He licked at the sore skin and started pressing wet kisses down the curve of my ass.

I should've told him what I was thinking. That the thought of him treating other women like this drove me to the point of distraction. But I didn't want him to think this was anything more than it was. If I confessed those thoughts, he'd label me as clingy or think I wanted this to be something it couldn't be. And that wasn't me. I didn't want or need him for anything other than sex. Those thoughts were just ... out of character.

"I was just wondering if I'd even feel it tomorrow morning."

Lucas hummed into my skin, not rising to my bait. Instead, his lips went lower and I turned my head to see him drop to his knees. Before my brain could put two and two together, Lucas' hands slid under me, pulling me by the thighs so my cunt met his lips.

I buried my face into his sheets and screamed his name. It was the least I could do to let him know my mind was nowhere else but here, with him tongue fucking me to heaven. The tip of his tongue swirled over my clit, quickly bringing me to the edge. And when I was shaking, just one push away from coming, Lucas' hand left my thigh and came down on my ass. Hard. And I came as the sting hit me, my body shaking before melting into the sheets. The only thing that held me in the here and now was Lucas' grip on my left thigh.

Even though I'd flattened into the bed, Lucas kept one hand on my thigh, angling me open so he didn't have to stop eating. The swipes of his tongue were torturous and I was on the verge of begging him to give my cunt a break when another smack resounded.

"Watching your ass bounce up close with your come on my lips has got me so fucking hard, Mia." Lucas stood behind me and I was too dazed to see what he was doing until I was draped over his lap. "I don't want to admit how long it's been since I could get this hard again, this fast, but it's all your doing. *You* do this to me. You and your tiny ass sports bras running all around my gym testing my control. Breaking me."

Lucas jerked his hips, pressing his come-covered cock into my stomach. I pushed up onto my elbows and looked at him over my shoulders. He was massaging my ass, tracing a reddening handprint. His cock twitched beneath me and suddenly the punishment wasn't exciting anymore. All I wanted was to be back on his cock.

"Lucas, I want –"

"You're not getting out of your punishment just because I'm desperate to get back inside you."

He was desperate? *I* was the desperate one. I couldn't stay still, the only things I could get out were whimpers, and my ass was on fire.

"Will my Princess' dirty little fantasies be fulfilled with a few more quick swats?" Lucas asked, finally looking up to meet my gaze. His eyes were dark, gray hair tugged in different directions. Wild, he looked wild and out of control.

I nodded and the motion was immediately followed by Lucas' hand landing on my ass. He kept his eyes on mine, even as I winced and jerked in his hold for the proceeding smacks. And his gaze was intense. I don't think anyone's ever looked at me so closely. Like he was watching for my limit, memorizing my reactions, and being hypnotized by me all at once.

He didn't move to different spots like he'd done before. Instead he focused on one spot, making sure I'd feel it tomorrow, be able to see his mark. And fuck I liked knowing I'd have that handprint tomorrow. Liked knowing that when I hanged, I'd be able to catch sight of it in the mirror.

With the spankings done, Lucas took me by the waist, yanking me around so I landed on his lap. My knees braced on either side of his hips and I tilted forward, wrapping my arms around his neck. Lucas' hands ran up my back, pressing my chest against him. Our heavy breaths rubbed my breast against his chest hair, making the skin itch. I wanted to move and create some space, but Lucas' eyes held me in place.

Without speaking, I knew what he wanted from me. And it certainly wasn't to move away from him.

I reached one hand between us and took hold of his wet cock, slowly stroking him. Lucas' head fell back and I kissed up his neck, enjoying the scrape of his scruff and the way he moaned and bucked his hips. My desire to get him back inside me was quickly overshadowed by my desire to watch his reactions. I can't remember the last time I watched someone this much during sex, but it was fascinating watching his constant frown dissolve into a groan of pleasure.

"Did I really break you, Lucas?" I whispered into his ear. Lucas' head snapped up and I pulled back to meet his gaze. Wild, I'd describe his look as wild. *I* did that to him.

"Yes, Mia, you did. What am I supposed to do after this, huh? Fuck my hand knowing nothing will be as good as *this*?" Lucas's hands moved to squeeze my ass, pulling me closer and lifting me up and down, dragging my clit along his shaft. "How am I supposed to act when I see you at work now that I know how you taste? How tight your cunt squeezes when you come?"

Lucas sped up his rocking and I let go of his dick to hold onto his shoulders. Lucas pulled me up, lifting me onto my knees. The head of his cock rested at my entrance, twitching in anticipation. I shivered in response, both to his words and the prospect of being full again.

"That sounds like a you problem." The words were far from convincing, coming out in a breathy sigh.

"I guess so. But you know what?" Lucas lowered my hips, slowly pushing his head inside me. He stopped there, his grip tightening when I tried to lower myself.

"Lucas," I whined.

"I know, princess, I know. But I need you to know I'm going to make this a you problem too." Lucas was quiet for a long moment, arms flexing as I pulsed around his head. And when he still didn't make a move, I gave up.

"Fine, how?"

"By finally giving this greedy little cunt what it needs."

Lucas pulled my hips down as he thrust into me, nearly splitting me in two. My body was on fire, burning and stinging and just so damn hot. The only thing I could manage to do was hold onto Lucas' neck as he impaled me on his cock.

His words echoed in my head with every slap of our skin. *I'm going to make this a you problem.* No, that couldn't happen. Once we were done, I would be over him. I didn't do repeats, let alone anything long-term, and I certainly didn't think about or pine after dudes I've already fucked. If he thought he could fuck me well enough to evoke those sorts of emotions, then he was insane. And I needed to regain control.

I braced my hands on Lucas' broad shoulders and he slowed to a halt.

"What do you want, Mia?" He pressed me against his chest again, nuzzling into my neck, licking and nibbling the sensitive skin.

"I want –" The words cut off in a breathy gasp when he started nibbling my ear.

"You'll get what you want, Princess. But first ..." Lucas' hand slid up my back, tangling into my hair and pulling me away just far enough so that my nipples still brushed against his chest hair. "First, I want to watch you use me. Take what you need from me, Mia. Use Daddy's cock to make yourself come."

Bastard. That's what I was going to say. Unfortunately, I was too damn hungry for my next orgasm to pout about it.

Gripping onto his shoulders, I shuffled my knees to pull myself up. I rose up until just his head was inside me, then slid back down as slowly as I could manage. Lucas tilted back, one hand bracing behind him and the other tightening on my hip.

Despite my growing need to come again, I kept my pace slow, enjoying the way Lucas groaned and his face twisted. Guess all those squats were finally paying off.

"Mia," Lucas growled my name, hand tightening in the sheets, brow furrowing. "Stop playing with me."

Lucas jerked his hips up, urging me into a faster pace. I squeezed his shoulders, fighting the urge to match his thrust.

"What are you doing to me, Princess?"

Making sure you're the one with the problem. Making sure you're the one who pines and lusts after we're done.

"I'm doing exactly what you told me to. I'm using Daddy's cock to make myself come."

Lucas chuckled and the hand on my hip trailed around my waist to my clit. He circled the bundle of nerves with quick, rough motions. My body moved on its own, quickening my pace to chase the high he'd triggered.

"That's it, Princess. Take what you need. Fuck me out of your system if you can." Lucas caught my protest with a kiss, pulling away while grazing my bottom lip between his. And with light pecks to the sting, he growled, "Just fuck me like you've been wanting to, like I've been dreaming about. No more thinking or stalling. *Fuck me.*"

I responded by riding him frantically because words couldn't describe that need burning inside me. Each time he whispered little words of praise and soft grunts of desperation, heat rushed through me, crashing at the point where his thumb still rubbed me into a tizzy. When my body started shaking and my movements stalled, Lucas jerked up, using the hand he'd been bracing on to rock me into another orgasm. I leaned into him, clinging to his neck as I tensed and burned.

Lucas moved his hand away from my clit and wrapped his arms around me. Everything tilted as he fell back, bringing me down to rest on his chest. He kissed along my hairline, starting to slowly thrust up into me. "What do you say, Princess? Are you satisfied?"

I hummed in reply, so exhausted and spent that there was nothing else I could possibly be but satisfied. But even so, as he started to chase his own release, the feel of his pelvis rubbing against my clit started another wave.

I pushed up against his chest, keeping one hand planted there while I reached behind me to cup his balls with the other. Lucas shook underneath me, his hands grabbing my hips tight enough to leave a mark. His cock twitched inside me and the knowledge I was driving him insane drove me closer to orgasming. And I want him to go with me.

I let go of his balls and leaned forward. Bracing myself with one arm by his head, I put a hand on his jaw, tilting his face to look at me. His eyes met mine and rather than let me speak, both his hands cupped my face and he brought our lips together. The kiss was sloppy, drool trickling down cheeks, teeth scraping against lips. It felt just as desperate as the sound of our hips slapping together.

"Come with me, Mia," Lucas whispered into my lips. His words had me tensing around his cock and his hips quickly stalled as he came. And when I joined him, my arms gave up and I collapsed against his chest. His arms wrapped around me, holding me as our breaths became even and our heart rates settled. And even then, I didn't particularly want to get up. Especially when he kissed the top of my head and his voice came out husky as he said, "That's my girl."

13

Lucas

For a moment when I woke up, I was satisfied. I'd gotten to fuck the woman I'd been obsessing over for weeks, gotten to see her come apart for me, and gotten more pleasure out of one night than I'd gotten in the past five years.

But then I rolled over in bed and she wasn't there.

She wasn't in bed or the bathroom or the living room or any other damn place in my condo.

Neither was there a note or even a fucking text.

She left with zero trace that she'd ever been there.

So with that sour start to the day, I went to work late after spending the morning moping at home and being mad at myself for accepting her stupid proposal. Get her out of my system. Who the fuck was I kidding? Keeping her in my bed for a week, a month wouldn't be enough for me to tire of that smart mouth and tight cunt.

And now I'd be haunted by the feel and taste of her for the rest of my life.

I pushed away from my desk and eyed the clock over my door. It was just about closing time, so Rick should be the only one here. I'll see if he needs anything and then I'll go home for a much-needed drink.

"Hey, boss, there's just one more person in the studio. Assuming she doesn't touch anything else, we're all set for closing," Rick said, popping his head into my office. Normally Rick didn't bother checking in with me unless it was a prelude to asking to go home early. And while I was desperately in need of a drink, I'd rather be alone as soon as possible.

"All right, I'll give them a reminder to wrap things up and take care of the rest. You're good to go, enjoy the rest of your evening."

Rick pumped his fist and ran off to the employee lounge. I took a deep breath and tried to remind myself how to talk to customers as I locked the front door before heading to the studio. One bad mood and a cross voice could result in angry reviews and loss of business and –

I stepped into view of the studio, the glass wall revealing exactly who was in there.

Mia was in her usual spot, back center against the wall, stretching, just like Rick had mentioned. She was facing away from the glass wall, doing a downward dog, pedaling her feet.

I wanted to yank down her pants and see if I'd left a mark on her ass. Wanted to bite down and leave one for good measure.

The fuck did this woman do to me?

I straightened and went to the door, knocking twice before I opened it. Mia didn't look up as I entered. Instead, she moved onto her knees, cat/cowing her back.

"I'll just be another minute, Rick. I know y'all are closing soon. I had a rough night, if you know what I mean. And I really need to stretch it out." Mia laughed, the sound soft and breathy and it made my nerves stand on end.

"So you're willing to joke about our night together when you can't even stay for breakfast?" The words came out harsh and I wasn't particularly sorry for it. Mia's back stiffened but she didn't turn her head to look at me.

"Lucas." She said my name like she was trying to sound unaffected, but I heard the strain, the hesitation, and saw her hands twitch as she pushed back into a child's pose. "I'll be out of your hair in a minute."

I didn't want her out of my hair. And I certainly didn't want her playing off our night together like this, like it was a joke.

"Was that your plan all along? To leave without a word?" I took slow steps towards her, not because I was waiting for her to tell me to go away, I knew she wouldn't, but so I could see the goosebumps spread across her shoulders and down her arms. She was in a black set today, the straps of her sports bras crisscrossing over her back to form little diamonds.

"I didn't see anything wrong with it. It was just a one-night thing," she murmured. She shuffled her knees further apart and deepened the stretch, tensing when I stopped behind her and knelt down.

"Right, one night to get each other out of our systems." Her breathing had gotten shallow on my approach and now she was shuffling in place. I leaned over her and braced my hands on either side of her, close, but not touching. And she stilled beneath me.

"So tell me, Mia, am I fucked out of your system now? Because I'm sure as hell not done with you." I grinded into her ass, letting her feel just how badly I wanted back inside her. "I had plans for you this morning and you leaving put me in a sour mood."

"That sounds like a you problem," she said, even as she started to grind against my cock.

"That line again, huh? I already told you I was going to make this your problem too. And if I haven't satisfied you enough to do that, then don't you think I owe you a few more orgasms?" I tangled my fingers into her hair and tugged until her head rested on its side. She kept her gaze forward, biting her bottom lip.

Dread started to seep in then. What if I was the only one interested in going back for more? What if she truly satisfied whatever desire she had? That meant I was just some old creep who wouldn't leave her alone.

I pushed away from Mia, readying myself to leave when her hand caught my wrist.

"I didn't say no," she huffed, the attitude I'd become familiar with finally returning.

"You didn't say yes, either."

Mia rolled her eyes before pulling so that I had to brace myself on my forearms. "Is there anybody else here?"

"There shouldn't be. Unless Rick forgot something." I didn't want anyone to know about Mia and me because of how it might affect the business. But Rick was close to Mia's age and could be a little flirtatious. If he just so happened to hear Mia crying out my name and effectively never flirted with Mia again, I wouldn't mind it.

"Okay," Mia paused, taking a deep breath before continuing, "Just one more time, then."

"Right. *Just* one more time," I repeated, already knowing I'd get her to say that as many times as I had to.

I pushed back up and started working her leggings and underwear down to her knees. She arched up to help, putting her bare ass right in my face. I hadn't spanked her hard enough last night to leave a mark, but I did leave a little hickey where I'd bit and sucked her ass cheek. I grazed my thumb over the irritated skin, satisfaction swelling my cock as I imagined leaving more marks, winding along her body, up to her neck where anyone could see that she was claimed, that she was *mine*.

Already feeling desperate, I snaked one arm around her chest and pulled her up against me. She quivered in my hold, the shaking turning violent when I cupped her pussy with my other hand.

"Were you really going to pretend you were done with me while your pussy was this wet?" I traced her entrance as I waited for the snarky comeback. But when it didn't come, I froze. "What's wrong, Mia?"

She tensed in my arms, then shrugged. I wasn't a fan of that answer.

Pushing her legs with my knees and holding her by the waist, I turned us until we were facing the wall of mirrors. Mia gasped, eyes fluttering to where my hands possessively held her against me. Her cheeks burned, the blush creeping down her neck.

"Are you getting shy on me, Princess?" I asked, kissing her neck and smothering myself in her scent.

"No," she said defiantly. "I'm just surprised you're willing to risk fucking in your precious gym. What if a customer finds out?"

"No one's going to know," I growled into her ear. "But I think it's cute that you tried to hide your shyness with an argument."

Mia huffed but finally looked up to meet my eyes in the mirror. "I'm just nervous."

"You weren't nervous when you kept talking about sex at dinner or when I finger fucked you in the middle of a restaurant. In fact, I'd say you had a bit too much confidence. So what's different about now?"

"It's easy to be confident when I know what I'm getting into, when I know what's coming."

"I'll show you who's coming," I chuckled, returning my hand to her cunt and slowly sliding two fingers in. She instantly pulsed around me. As I thrust my fingers, I slid my free hand up her bra and freed her right breast to knead and pinch her nipple. Mia's head fell back against my shoulder and she started moving her hips to ride my fingers.

"Did you go home, crawl into your lonely bed, and think of me?" She nodded, gasping out my name as I pushed in another finger, fucking her harder. "And did you fuck yourself with the memory of how good my cock felt inside you?"

"Lucas, please," she whined, already so worked up that she was spilling over my hand. Had she been craving me since she left? Her pussy crying out for my cock even when the woman herself was too stubborn to admit she wanted me.

"Please what?"

"Fuck me, Daddy."

Never in my life have I gotten my pants down quicker. And it still wasn't quick enough.

When I slid inside her, we both let out long sighs of relief. I took a moment to relax so I didn't have to immediately pull out and come. But Mia didn't give me much time to adjust. She dropped her hands to the floor and started pushing her ass into me, fucking herself on my cock with no regard for how close I was to coming already.

"Mia, slow down," I grounded out, taking a tight hold of her hips and holding them in place with my cock buried inside her. I let one hand go to grab her ponytail and pulled until her eyes met mine in the mirror. Watching each other had an immediate effect on our bodies, both of us twitching in anticipation. So I made the decision that since this would be far from the last time I'll fuck Mia, this one can be quick.

"Don't take your eyes off the mirror," I instructed, letting go of her hair when she nodded. She kept her eyes on me as I started thrusting into her, but then her eyes flitted to look at herself, her half-free tits and wild hair. It was an intoxicating image. She took one hand to her clit, circling herself a few times before reaching further to massage my balls.

Her touch made my body feel like an incendiary. Everything burned and the only thought I had was to pound into her until she came. I swatted her hand away from my balls and started rubbing her clit, finding the pace based on how much her arms started to shake.

When her hips failed to meet my thrusts, I pulled out. Mia instantly whined until I filled her with my fingers, pushing and rubbing against her G-spot as I stroked myself between her ass cheeks. Her cries and moans and the way she squeezed my fingers as she orgasmed had me coming all over her ass, drops dotting her lower back and dripping down her sides.

"You're coming home with me tonight." I met Mia's gaze in the mirror and she nodded, her eyes dazed and a relaxed smile pulling up her lips. "And you're staying till morning this time."

14

Lucas

The last few weeks have been the most relaxing days I've had in a long, long time. Maybe from before I even opened the gym. And it was all because of Mia.

The only thing that ruined it was the way Mia kept herself closed off. She was more than open about the things she wanted me to do with her body, but when it came to her as a person, taking care of her, and knowing more about her family and interests, she quickly turned it down with the excuse that we were nothing more than fuck buddies.

Fuck buddies. That's what she called our relationship. The term grated against me. I might have a hard time picturing us having a future with the age gap and the image I needed to maintain for the gym's success, but I'd never label what was going on between us with some bullshit, social media lingo title.

Despite being in the middle of a staff meeting, I checked my phone when my manager took the floor to talk about upcoming schedule changes we'd discussed earlier. I'd left Mia in my bed nearly five hours ago and she still hasn't replied to a single text. Her lack of response agitated my already irritated nerves. The way she kept herself distant from me made every small thing feel like the end. Like she'd just up and vanish when I wasn't looking because she got bored of fucking me.

I restarted my phone to ensure it wasn't some mechanical error and when that yielded nothing, I decided I'd stop by her apartment after work.

15

Mia

"Mia?" Lucas' voice called from somewhere outside the bedroom. Even though his volume was relatively soft, the sound grated against my head like nails on a chalkboard. I turned onto my stomach and pulled a pillow over my head, trying to block out every possible irritant.

I should've known this was coming. Migraines were always the first sign of PMS and I was due in just under a week. I should've gotten up with my alarm and made sure I had enough food and water and caffine. But Lucas' bed was so comfy and I didn't have work or a gym class, so I just let myself relax into the comfort of his scent.

And now that decision came back to bite me in the ass.

Even with my head buried under the pillow, eyes tightly closed, I could still see the floating black spots.

"Mia?" Lucas called again, this time with a knock on the door. Since sound and light and movement all hurt, I didn't respond. And instead of understanding that no response meant I needed to be left alone, Lucas stepped into the bedroom.

He said my name again and I threw the pillow towards his voice. Unfortunately, the act made the nausea worse, and, based on the sound the pillow made when it landed, I don't think it hit him.

"Mia, what's wrong?" Lucas' footsteps headed towards the bed, paused to presumably pick up the pillow, then came to sit beside me. His hand rested on my back, rubbing up and down my spine, soothing my irritation.

It was so stupid how calm his touch could make me. No one should have that kind of easy sway over me.

"I'm fine, I just need some sleep," I mumbled.

"Is that not what you've been doing since I left?" I imagined him raising an eyebrow at me. "Because if you haven't been sleeping, then you'll need to come up with another excuse as to why you haven't texted me or Carrie back all day."

"All day? Carrie?" My thoughts ping-ponged so much that it hurt.

"It's past five, Princess." He must've noticed the way I flinched at the sound of our voices because he lowered his tone to just above a whisper. The perfect volume for my bogged-down mind. "I stopped by your place after work because ... you never answered your phone. Carrie said you hadn't replied to her either."

"It hurts to look at my phone," I murmured, deciding the guilt of not responding would be worse than admitting I'd been curled up all day, practically dying while I failed to fall back asleep.

"Because of a migraine?"

God fucking damn it, Carrie.

"I'm fine, I just need to sleep it off." I turned away from Lucas, his hand trailing off my back.

"You're clearly not fine. Now, Carrie gave me your medicine, but she also said you probably haven't eaten anything all day. Is that true?"

That uncomfortable itch I always got when Carrie tried to mom me was suffocating now. Why did people feel the need to intervene? I'm fine, I don't need anyone to take care of me. I didn't need it as a kid, I sure as hell didn't need it now.

"Mia?" Lucas prodded, hand returning to my back. That touch that was so soothing minutes ago now had the same feeling as grinding my teeth. I jerked away, away from his touch and that uncomfortable smothering feeling.

"I'm fine," I repeated, gritting the words out as loudly as I could manage to get the point across. "I call you Daddy because of the gray hair, not because I need you to take care of me. So you can just leave me alone."

The bed shifted as Lucas stood then walked out. And for a moment, everything was quiet. Until my brain wanted to think of everything all at once at the highest possible volume. I turned onto my stomach, curled into a ball, and tried to massage away the pain.

I knew the only thing that would really help would be something in my stomach, meds, and a nice hot shower featuring an orgasm or two. But I could barely turn onto my side without nausea sloshing all the contents of my stomach. If I could just outlast the nausea, I could take care of everything else.

I stayed in Lucas' room for several long minutes, exhausted beyond all belief and still unable to fall asleep. I wonder how much longer it'll be until Lucas comes to bed for the evening? Hopefully, he didn't get all uppity like Carrie did when I told her off. But if he was mad about it, so what? That just meant our time fucking each other was over. Fine. I didn't care. This relationship was just about getting each other out of our systems anyways. Just because that was taking longer than I originally thought, didn't mean –

The smell of warm bread made my stomach gurgle. The sound irritated my head but it was the first time the very concept of food sounded appealing.

Just as I was about to scrounge up the energy to sit up, Lucas stepped into the bedroom with three crescent rolls in hand. As Lucas made his way to sit beside me, I slowly sat up, cradling my head to ease the pain. When I was upright, I reached a hand out to the rolls but Lucas pulled away.

"I'll keep this quick because I know you're in pain, but I know you don't *need* me to take care of you. But I want to. Will you let me?"

Maybe this was actually the worst migraine I'd ever had because I was considering saying yes. Over the years plenty of people had said they didn't mind helping me out for one thing or another, but nobody ever said they *wanted* to care for me. And that one stupid word made a world of difference.

"Okay," I murmured weakly, partly because of the migraine, but mostly because even though I could believe he actually wanted to help, it still felt ... uncomfortable, like wearing a turtleneck for the first time.

"Okay?" Lucas repeated, his brow raised like he didn't believe me. Which was fair, but I was far from in the mood to further expand on why I was accepting his help now. So instead I just reached for the rolls again and this time Lucas set them in my hand. I took slow bites, relishing the warmth of the bread, while Lucas wrapped himself around me and then pulled me back to rest my head against his chest. He stroked my arm as I ate, the motion so soothing I could almost fall asleep.

Once I'd finished the rolls, Lucas shuffled to pull something out of his pocket. My bottle of extra strength, migraine Excedrin. And I knew it was mine because I'd scribbled an M on the lid so Carrie wouldn't use my meds up, like she did the first month we roomed together. I was what some might call a petty bitch.

She must've given them to Lucas just in case. I was irritated but grateful.

I slowly scooped out two pills, trying to make as little noise as possible, while Lucas reached over to grab his bedside waterbottle. Pills taken, I nestled back into Lucas' chest, taking slow breaths as I visualized the drugs in my system like *Osmosis Jones*. The little guys would blast away the tar-like amoebas that were clawing the inside of my head.

"All right, what's next?"

"Huh?"

"Carrie said you get migraines a lot, so I assume you have a routine. What's next?"

"Shower," I murmured, dragging myself to the edge of the bed before Lucas put a hand on my shoulder. I waited as he stood, rounded the bed, and scooped me up into his arms.

"Pretty strong for an old guy. You know I can still walk, right?"

"Glad to see your attitude is back. But I saw you wince every time you so much as shifted. I don't like the idea of letting you hurt yourself when I'm perfectly capable of carrying you." Lucas stepped into the bathroom and set me on the counter. "Besides, you're not docile like this often, I might as well take advantage of it."

"Hmm, I like when you take advantage of me."

"I don't need to take advantage when you freely climb on my cock every morning."

I'd have rolled my eyes if I didn't think it would hurt.

Lucas turned on the shower, holding his hand under the spray until he was satisfied with the temperature. Then he motioned for me to stand and undressed me. I stood, stunned, only moving when he gestured me to, trying to process what this moment was doing to my brain, which still felt like a fire alarm was going off. There was never a time in my life when someone took my clothes off so gently, especially without the intention of fucking me after. And Lucas was watching me so closely. Like he was waiting for me to shut him down like I admittedly always did.

It's not that I didn't want to tell him about my shit parents that weren't capital T traumatizing, but still shit. But when people ask after your family, they want things like what they did for a living, where they lived, shitty things I didn't care about because my parents weren't worth caring for. And that wasn't the kind of thing you tell a fuck buddy. ... a title Lucas seemed to genuinely hate.

"You're gonna make your migraine worse if you keep thinking that hard." Lucas' thumb stroked my furrowed brow then glided down to my chin to angle me up so I was looking at him. Fuck. I was feeling very vulnerable.

"I don't like my family." It was a tiny truth. Like the tip of an iceberg. But sharing that little piece of truth with Lucas felt good.

Lucas took a moment, eyes fluttering across my face before saying, "Keep saying things like that and I really will feel like I'm taking advantage of you like this."

I huffed a laugh as Lucas put the last of my clothes aside and guided me into his amazing shower. Equipped with a waterfall head, a detachable nozzle, and a deep bench perfect for sitting under the water for hours or other fun activities. Honestly, I'd fuck Lucas solely for access to his shower, especially for migraine days when the only thing that soothed my pain was a hot shower.

I settled onto the bench, rested my head against the wall, and closed my eyes as the water washed over me.

"Stand up for a second."

My eyes shot open to see Lucas step into the shower with me, closing the door behind him. Too confused and tired to question his command, I stood. He took my spot on the bench, then pulled me into place between his legs. I didn't really see the point of him joining me, but I had to admit I liked the feel of his skin against mine. It wasn't until the pop of a bottle that I realized what he'd intended.

"Lucas, you don't have to –"

"I know," he interrupted, squirting out some of the shampoo I've left here and sudsing it up.

"But I don't really need –"

"I know. But I want to. Besides, washing up can help you feel better, even if it's just mentally." Lucas started massaging the soap into my scalp, deep, small circles that relieved so much pressure. We sat in silence as he washed me, the only sound the water and the shuffling of our bodies as Lucas moved me around to wash and rinse different parts of me.

If you had asked me to picture Lucas washing me up, it would've come with a lot of possessive grabbing and certain spots getting all the attention. Instead, his touch was soft, gliding over my body without lust. And while his hands behaved, a certain appendage didn't get the memo.

"Lucas, are you –"

"I am. Caring for you, getting to do something you won't let anyone else do, is having a stronger effect on me than I anticipated. And if I knew it wouldn't hurt you, I'd bend you over this bench and reward you for being such a good girl and letting Daddy take care of you."

Heat flooded my insides and suddenly I very much wanted Lucas gone so I could continue to the orgasm part of my migraine routine.

After rinsing the last bit of soap, Lucas wrapped his arms around me and pulled me up against his chest. When he spoke, the words tickled against my neck and set off a trail of goosebumps. "Once you're feeling better, I'll …" His words fell away like he was lost in thought. And when I turned to look at him, to see what exciting thing he might have planned, he held me in place. "Unless you've got another step on your migraine routine, I'll let you relax here while I go fix us some dinner. Does anything sound good?"

Lucas lifted me by the waist and set me back down to his right so he could stand. He turned to me, cock right in my face. It took me a few long, *long*, seconds to respond.

"Oh yeah, I'll stay here for … a bit. But um, maybe you could pick up some Chinese? Pork fried rice sounds really good right now."

"Is there something else I can do to make you feel better?" Lucas asked with a raised eyebrow. Yeah, no, I definitely didn't want to tell him about my plans and have him feel obligated to try and get me to orgasm without moving my head. Honestly, just the idea of sex was nauseating at the moment, but that rush of endorphins was calling my name.

"No. I'm just gonna sit in here until the food gets here."

"Mia." Lucas leaned into me, bracing his hands on either side of my hips. "I can tell when you need to come."

"I can take care of that myself, thank you. I'm not exactly capable of reciprocating at the moment and excessive movement would hurt anyways. So your involvement is unnecessary."

Lucas' eyes narrowed.

"Didn't we just have this conversation?" He reached over me and pulled down a … hand towel? I mean, I could get into some more intense spanking sessions but … Then he tossed it on the floor with a splash and knelt down. "As we just established, I get off taking care of you. So I don't need you to reciprocate. And I can make you come without too much movement. Just sit back and relax, Princess."

Lucas pushed my knees apart and settled himself between my thighs. He didn't waste any time, immediately leaning in and licking the length of my cunt. And there was no use arguing against that.

My hands found his hair, tangled in and pulled him closer. He took that as a sign to kick it up, sucking my clit into his mouth. Heat instantly shook through my body. I let my head rest against the wall, enjoying the way his tongue twisted around my clit between sucks, then dipped into my cunt, humming in satisfaction.

Meanwhile, all I could manage to say was his name, in soft little whimpers that seemed to keep Lucas going. I couldn't even bring myself to call him Daddy at the moment. That term was for when this was all sex and … it wasn't anymore. I was never going to fuck this man out of my system, in fact, he'd set roots in me, roots that were starting to erode the discomfort of being cared for.

He was mine now, he had to be.

And that was the last coherent thought I had before I came on Lucas' mouth. My breathing was hard and my heart was pounding. Lucas kept his mouth on me, his touch gentle as he licked away my come. When he was satisfied, he stood and braced one hand on the wall over me while the other hand gripped his cock.

"Keep your eyes on me." He started stroking himself and my eyes dipped from his face to his cock and want hit so hard, I reached up without thinking.

"No." My hand wrapped around his wrist, stopping his motions, and I looked back up at him. "I want you to fuck me."

Lucas bit his lip and his breath started to become shallow as his eyes trailed over my body. Without a word, Lucas pulled me up and into his arms. We stood there for a moment, Lucas stroking my hair, cock pressed against my stomach. Then he grunted, moving to turn off the shower. He stepped out, quickly wiping down, wrapping the towel around his waist. If I was less horny and didn't still have a slight ache at my temples, I'd have laughed at the way his cock stood under the towel.

Continuing his grumpy silence, Lucas took my hand, gently tugging me out of the shower. He snagged another towel off the bar and started drying me off with intense focus. In fact, he was looking at my body with such focus, I started to squirm. "What're you thinking?"

"I'm thinking it'd be better for both of us if I wanted you less. You tell me to fuck you and I can't do anything else. You tell me to fuck you and even though I know you're in pain, I don't give a damn because my body was waiting for that permission. I *need* you, Mia. And I wish I needed you less."

"I don't." The words were out of my mouth like it was an instinct to say them. Lucas looked down at me, the towel slipping from his hands. He held my eyes as he undid his towel, letting it join mine on the floor.

"Is that something you say to all your fuck buddies?" he asked, stepping closer. Guess that label really pissed him off. I should make it up to him when I'm feeling better.

"No." I pushed up on my toes and pressed a soft kiss to his cheeks, not hating how vulnerable I felt with this man right now.

As soon as I settled back on my feet, Lucas scooped me up in a princess hold and carried me to bed. He settled me on my stomach and wasted no time climbing on top of me and positioning the head of his cock against my cunt. He leaned down, arms braced on either side of my head, and nipped at my ear. "One more thing, Princess. Last time you had a migraine and took care of yourself. Who were you thinking of?"

"You know who," I murmured, trying to push my ass up so he'd push into me. He just chuckled and pulled away.

"Glad to know you're feeling better. But it doesn't matter if I know who, I need to hear you say it."

"You," I whined, voice soft and needy. "It's been you for a while."

"That's my good girl," he whispered as he slid into me.

Having him slide into me, *finally* filling me after hours of pain, made my whole body relax. Like having this man fuck me with slow strokes, was exactly what my body needed to recover.

And that was the final straw, I couldn't ignore what I felt or wanted from Lucas anymore.

16

Lucas

Rick was telling me something about his upcoming schedule change and I didn't hear a damn word of it because Mia just stepped out of class. Ever since she let me care for her during her migraine and subsequent cramping days, things had been different. It didn't feel like she was holding her tongue as much. We hadn't revisited what she'd said about her parents or the dance studio, but I could wait for those big things. For now, I was just grateful she'd told me more specifics about her ankle injury. And that she was finally wearing a shirt around the gym again.

"Sorry, Rick, I've gotta talk with Mia." He gave me an odd look but didn't say anything. I was getting to the point where I didn't give a shit what anyone at the gym thought about Mia and me. In fact, there were a few men in particular that I wanted to know Mia was mine solely based on the way their eyes followed her through the gym.

"Is that a hickey, young lady?" Judy teased and Mia's hand immediately went up to cover the mark I'd left last night. I'd watched her cover it up this morning, holding in a complaint, but I was glad to see the makeup didn't hold through her class. "I bet it's a younger man, huh? They're insatiable, aren't they?"

The comment pulled at a nagging thread. If she thought that was the mark of a man younger than Mia, what would she think knowing it was me? Anxiety clawed at my insides, battling the desire to mark my territory. I'm not sure which was the bigger beast.

"Yup, younger guys sure are a handful," Mia said with a laugh. The comment made my skin burn and itch. We might not have said things out loud, but she was mine and she knew it. Trying to pass off my mark as some younger man's was unacceptable.

"Mia." Her name came out growled, far angrier than I'd intended. Judy's eyes widened, looking between me and Mia, who sucked in a deep breath. "I'd like to ask you about our social media. Do you have a moment to talk in my office?"

It was an excuse I'd come up with right after we spoke for the first time, the start of a scenario that played every time I sought some relief before I finally had her. And just like she did in those fantasies, Mia smiled, knowing exactly what would happen behind closed doors.

Except this wasn't my fantasy. I was pissed at the thought of people thinking Mia was anybody's but mine. And if this ended in sex, it'd be for me to claim her.

As soon as the door clicked behind Mia, I had her pressed up against it, smothering her gasp with a kiss. I pushed all my anger and frustration at her and she accepted, tilting and opening for me.

"What's this about a younger man?" I growled when I was finally able to tear myself off her.

"I was covering for you. You've been too obvious lately, everybody's gonna think you're a horn dog going after some young ass. Pretty sure that'd drive away customers." She murmured the excuse, her voice breathy from more than just the kiss.

"But is there?" I gripped her waist and hiked her up the door, pinning her in place with my hips. She instantly grinded against me, eyes fluttering closed.

"Is there what?" she murmured, voice soft.

"Is there a younger man? Someone you'd rather be with? Someone else you're seeing?" This is where the generational divide might break us. Her generation dated around before committing to one person, mine stuck with one at a time. In the back of my mind, I knew that was just an assumption, that it was likely untrue. But it was too prevalent in my brain to let go of, especially when the thought of Mia with anybody else made me want to burn everything.

"I've been with you, like, every night. Where would I find the time?"

"Mia, I'll ask you one more time. And you better have the right answer for me, princess, because my patience is wearing thin. Are you seeing anyone else?" When she didn't reply immediately, I dug my fingers in her ass, nudging her for a response.

"No." She said the word so quietly, I thought I imagined it. But when I met her eyes and saw that gleam of vulnerability she'd shown me before, I knew it was real.

"And why not?" I couldn't tell if my heart had stopped or if it was going too fast to recognize. Mia squirmed against me, biting at her lip before looking up at me.

"I don't want to."

"Why?"

"Because I want you. For more than just sex."

Everything went blank. I couldn't think, let alone process anything other than the fact that Mia was mine. She wanted me, despite our age gap, despite the clash of our attitudes, she *wanted me*. And I need her to feel exactly what that meant to me.

I slid my arm under her ass and carried her to my desk, setting her down in front of it so I could work her leggings off. Thank fuck she'd just come from barre and didn't have any shoes on. Once the pants were gone, I pulled her up onto the desk and stepped between her legs. I tried to slow myself down by running my fingers up and down her thighs, but Mia caught my right hand and brought it to her aching pussy.

"So wet for me," I murmured, sliding my fingers into her and curling. Mia arched her back, pushing into me.

"I guess I have a thing for possessive displays of jealousy." Her arms wrapped behind my head and I leaned into her neck to start marking the other side. "But why hickeys? They're so ... old school."

keys? They're so ... old school." "I needed to mark what's mine. You run around this gym in those tight-ass leggings and that scrap of fabric you call a bra. People look. *Men* look. I sure as hell was looking, lusting, before we even spoke. And since I can't just up and declare this as a women only gym, I need to make sure anyone looking knows you're unavailable, knows you're mine." I puncture the claim by biting just above her collar bone. Mia gasped, hips stalling, and for a moment, I'd thought I'd gone too far. That this sort of claiming was too intense, especially if we counted this as the start of our real relationship. But then her fingers dug into my hair and pulled until I was looking at her.

"What about you?"

"What?"

"People look at you too, other women. I was looking before too. How do I make sure they know you're taken?"

Oh, my sweet Princess, I don't think another woman could catch my eye if she tried.

But I didn't tell her that. It wasn't what she'd been asking for. Instead, I picked her up and settled us on my chair. I leaned my head to the side and pulled at the hem of my neckline.

"Mark me as yours then, princess." Her lips met my skin eagerly. The motions were hesitant at first, more kissing than sucking. But when I reached between us to pull out my cock, she sucked hard and then suddenly stopped.

"It's not gonna be a good look. You know, for the gym."

"If it's between losing a few customers and losing you …" I let my words trail off as I positioned my cock at her opening and lowered her down onto me. Mia gasped, forehead resting on my shoulder as she pulsed around me, hot squeezes that made me shudder. "Do you really need to ask which I'd choose?"

Mia didn't respond with words. She responded by bouncing on my cock, her hips moving at a deliciously fast pace. Then she resumed marking my neck, switching between nipping and sucking the tender skin and licking the sting.

"That's it, Mia. Make sure everyone knows who I belong to." I gripped her waist, keeping her impaled on my cock and grinding into me. Her lips left my skin with a heavy sigh.

"How's it look, Princess?" Mia lifted her head and I tilted mine so she'd have a good look in the dim office light. A coy smile tugged her lips up and she hummed in approval. The noise did something to me. Clicked something into place that's been growing ever since Mia called me out for running a class poorly. She might've frustrated me at times, driven me mad, and made me crawl over her walls to get to her heart, but she was mine now. Attitude and all.

"You wanna buy me a pill after this, Daddy? Or would you rather –"

"Yes," I growled, pulling her up and slamming her back down. Mia giggled, gripping my shoulders and readjusting her legs so she could ride me the way she liked and use me the way she needed. And knowing she was getting her pleasure, knowing she thought of me as hers, made everything tighten and burn. "That's right, Mia, take what's yours. Take it now."

I moved my hand to her back, pressing her to me, and took her mouth to mine. The clashing of our lips ushered our orgasms and I was only aware of her touch and the fire it brought.

We stayed silent for a long moment, both of us softly stroking the other's hair, relaxed, at home in each other's embrace. That was until a knock sounded on my door and Mia tensed in my arms.

"On a call, be out in a moment," I answered, praying that whoever was at the door didn't try to open it because I certain didn't have the peace of mind to make sure it was locked beforehand.

When a mumbled affirmative sounded and the shadow moved away, I stood, still holding on to Mia. I set her on the desk, grabbed a few tissues, and put them underneath us before pulling away from her. Once we were both cleaned up, as well as tissues could manage, I helped her redress and took her hand.

"Just gotta stop by the front desk before we go home."

When we left my office, Mia's hold on my hand dropped but I held tight. She looked up at me with a raised eyebrow, but I didn't answer the unasked question. I wanted people to know and I was done denying that want.

At the front desk, Rick was talking with a customer but turned when we entered the corner. His brow furrowed as his eyes found our entangled hands and I held my breath, waiting for a comment. But instead, Rick just shrugged it off.

"Hey boss man, do you mind if I switch shift times with Alex on Thursday?"

"Not a problem. Just make sure you put it up on the board. I'm about to go, but can you do something for me?" I took a breath, readying myself to confirm what Rick might have only just assumed based on our held hands. "Cancel Mia's account."

"What?" Rick and Mia said in unison, to varying degrees of confusion. I turned to Mia, ignoring her glare and outrage, and kissed her forehead.

"My girlfriend's not paying for a membership at my gym."

17

Mia

I didn't want to answer the phone. One, I hated talking on the phone because when it got quiet, I hung up and most people I knew didn't exactly like that trait. Two, because I hadn't spoken to the caller in years. Well, two years. Since I'd wrecked my ankle and had to quit dancing.

"Are you going to answer that?" Lucas asked. My phone wasn't ringing, but the screen was lit with Lily's picture and name.

"She was one of my friends from the dance studio," I said since I hadn't decided what to do yet. Lucas shifted closer to me on the couch and swiped a finger over my screen to answer the call. Asshole.

"Mia!" Lily screamed through the phone. I'd almost forgotten how chipper she was. It made for one hell of a contrast when we hung out. But despite our differences, we'd been close once. She was the sunshine to my grumpiness, a fair balance. Until my injury made me stop dancing and I got … extra sulky and unable to tolerate her perkiness. So I pulled away and our relationship naturally crumbled.

Part of me wanted to blame her for our friendship falling apart. She didn't exactly reach out and it's not like I could go back to the studio. But then I remembered how pessimistic and unpleasant I must've been to hang out with and I couldn't fault her. Or maybe she just thought I needed space. Lil was thoughtful like that.

"Hey, Lil, what's up?" Beside me, Lucas raised an eyebrow. We'd been officially dating for a month now and he had oh so gently encouraged me to talk about my dancing and family and all that trauma I refused to share before. And by gently, I mean he withheld sex from me when I refused to answer when he brought up my dancing again. It was probably the healthiest thing a man has ever done for me.

"Mia, Mia, Mia, a bunch of us from the studio are going to the Homesick Serenade concert tonight but Max and Fran are sick and I thought maybe you'd wanna take their tickets? Your roommate can come too! It's gonna be me, Dean, Corey, Annie, and Maya. Annie's Maya's new girl." Lily's voice was that kind of excited and anxious combo that made you feel like a dick if you said no. Like maybe she had to work up the nerve to call me.

But I actually didn't want to say no this time. Homesick was one of my favorite bands, at least my favorite currently touring band, and there'd been a guest singer at their last show and everyone was speculating if she was a new member or not. Her voice sounded like it was *meant* to be there. It was a whole thing.

And it was entirely possible that trauma dumping onto Lucas might have helped me get to the place where I could say yes. Turns out talking about your emotions and letting people in was actually good for you, who knew?

"I'm down, but for the other ticket could ..." I put my hand over the speaker and held it away. "Would you wanna go to a concert tonight?"

So far, our relationship mostly featured hanging out in quiet spaces. The bedroom, his office, the back of restaurants where nobody could see us or how Lucas' hand moved under the table. But we hadn't interacted with anyone as a couple outside of the gym. And I highly doubted their reactions were a good reflection of real-world strangers who didn't feel the need to be polite.

A concert would be different, public. We'd get all the judgmental glares and snide comments that made us hesitant to get together in the first place.

Plus this kind of concert wasn't exactly Lucas' thing. Especially on a work night. It'd be loud and crowded and more people my age or younger. I couldn't even picture him there, let alone having fun.

And it's not like I needed him to come along. We can do our own things and him not being there would make things a lot stressful but ... I was nervous to be around Lily and the rest. I wanted Lucas there as a comfort and buffer in case things went wrong.

Lucas bit at his lip and I could see the battle in his eyes. This was too far out of his comfort zone, I knew it. He was going to say no. And I don't know why it was so upsetting to think of him saying no, but it was. God damn, Lucas was turning me into a spoiled princess, wasn't he?

"Okay."

"Really?" I asked, at a definitely not higher pitch than normal.

"Don't sound so surprised. I'm not so old that a concert is unappealing. Especially if I'm going with a pretty girl." Lucas pulled at my arm until I was resting against him and kissed my cheek.

I rolled my eyes and returned the phone to my ear. "Sorry. Would you mind if I bring my boyfriend instead?"

"Boyfriend? Yeah, for sure! Can't wait to meet him. And see you! It's been so, so, so long! This is gonna be so much fun! I'll text you all the details for meeting up and stuff." And with a few more excited squeals, Lily hung up. It only took a few minutes for the text with several exclamation points and emojis to come in. We wouldn't have much time to get ready, but I was starting to get excited for the night.

"You didn't say anything about my age," Lucas remarked, placing an arm around my shoulders and pulling me against him.

"I don't think I need to."

Lucas was quiet for a moment before he finally asked, "And is that because you don't feel the need to explain yourself or because you've dated older men before?"

I snapped around and narrowed my eyes at Lucas. His face was stern set, like this was a question he'd been waiting to ask. And that stung, irritated all the old wounds that I thought were healing. He knew I didn't date before him and he knew why. He didn't exactly go through his dating history for me. For all I knew, he had dated someone younger before and that's why he was so hesitant to fuck me.

And despite our nice health chat about my trauma, I was still a bit of a brat with a jealous streak. So instead of giving him the honest answer, the one I would have thought he already knew, I stood and said, "Who's to say?"

Lucas called for me, but I walked straight to his room. If he got to ask questions that felt wrong to ask, I could too.

By the time I had pulled out the sex blanket and pillow, Lucas was at the door, arms crossed, brow furrowed. I tossed the items at his feet and raised an eyebrow but didn't say anything. Lucas waited for a moment, not breaking eye contact until he realized this was something I was going to be stubborn about and he sighed, rubbing the bridge of his nose.

"Fine, I'll ask. What is this about?" He asked, gesturing to the items at his feet.

"The same thing your question was about."

Lucas' chest rose in sharp waves, but he didn't move otherwise. I was so used to him scooping me up or pressing me up against a wall when we argued, that the lack of action felt like a drastic difference.

"I don't think it's unreasonable for me to ask about how our age difference is going to be perceived by your friends." Lucas' jaw ticked and the action didn't spur me into being a brat like usual either. In fact, it reminded me of how I acted when there was something I didn't want to talk about. And if I had to talk about my feelings, it was only fair he did too.

"Tell me what you're really feeling and I'll explain the blanket on the floor." I plopped back onto the bed and gestured for him to come closer. Lucas sighed but stepped up so he stood between my legs.

"I don't like the idea of being one of many, not with you." He took my face in his hands, gently stroking my cheeks. "The thought of you flitting around with older men all the time drives me insane. I ... I want to be the exception for you. Like you are for me."

Tell him. The words echoed in my head like they were coming from somewhere deep, deep from inside. Except that thought wasn't sounding so deep recently. It was nagging on me, threatening to leak out. But seeing as I'd never said those three words to anyone and the last time I'd said them to my parents it was brushed off like it meant nothing, I was a little nervous. And I just ... didn't know how to say it.

I was tempted to just fucking Google it. Surely there was a Wiki-How article on how to say those three words out loud at just the right moment so you get them said back instead of some pitying look.

But for right now, all I could manage was, "You are the exception. Both in age and in willingness to date. I would've thought you knew that already."

"I might've been able to put two and two together. But that logic doesn't make the wondering stop. I needed to hear it straight from you." Lucas' finger grazed over my cheek and to my lips. I reached up, hooking my finger through the loops of his jeans, and tugged him closer.

"The feeling's mutual. I don't like the idea of you being with a bunch of young chicks, replacing them whenever they get too old for you. Buying them special blankets and pillows for sex." There was a smidge more hurt than sarcasm than I intended and Lucas caught it. He pulled from my hold and knelt down.

"I can't even remember when I bought them, let alone who for. But I can remember the way you moved the blanket to grab my sheets when I spanked you for the first time. Did it bother you back then too?"

I huffed, turning away from Lucas. He chuckled and reached up to cup my cheek before repeating what I'd said moments ago, "Tell me what you're feeling."

"That you should buy a special blanket just for me," I snarked, but the bite wasn't there. Lucas smiled, pulling me into a kiss before standing. He took my hand, pulling me up and flesh against his body. Like with all our arguments, Lucas was hard, pushing against my stomach and that was all it took for heat to spread through me. If we hurried ...

"I know what you're thinking, but we don't have time. You have to get ready and I have to do some online shopping. Maybe if you're a good girl at the concert, I'll reward you later tonight."

"Oh yeah? And how exactly do I prove I'm a good girl, Daddy?"

"By making sure every man there knows your mine."

Our relationship was safe like this, inside a little game we played to get each other off. I didn't have to push things further. Not yet.

18

Lucas

I felt out of place. At the concert, with Mia's friends, at her side. And I wasn't the only one who thought so.

The moment we stepped into the crowded parking lot, heads turned to us with looks that ranged from questioning to disgust. No one said anything, but I could read it in their glares. They said I had no business being with Mia, that she was with me for the money, that they could show her a better time than some old man.

At least those later thoughts held no ground. We might've not had time for a full session before leaving, but I couldn't very well mark her neck without making her come, even if it was only around my fingers. And the sound of her crying out was all that was keeping me sane when men ogled her and others gave me dirty looks.

I had more pressing things to worry about than strangers judging me though. Mia's friends, or ex-friends, were chatting a mile a minute and I was struggling to keep up with the conversation. From what Mia told me, she pushed these people away after her ankle nearly shattered. They reminded her of what she couldn't do anymore and Mia wasn't exactly one to hold onto relationships when they got hard. So they fell out of touch. And while Mia didn't say it, I could tell she felt left behind.

I wouldn't let that happen again.

Except there seemed like nothing to worry about in that regard. Mia was smothered by Maya and Lily as soon as we walked up. While they occupied

Mia, I introduced myself to the others. Dean and Annie were Lily and Maya's partners and Corey was one of the few male dancers at the studio, a fact he seemed to be very proud of and repeated often.

If any of them thought badly of me being with Mia, they didn't show it. There was a brief moment of raised brows but when the looks didn't morph into anything judgmental, I began to relax. Or relax as much as I could be around a group of people 20 years younger than me. The conversation immediately shifted to the band and I quickly lost pace, even when Maya and Lily released Mia and they joined the rest of the group.

I tried to add to the conversation, but I felt out of place and even when I could think of something to add, I doubted if it was even relevant. So I kept quiet, wrapping my arms around Mia's waist and having her rest against my chest. Other than feeling out of place, it wasn't that bad. As long as Mia was leaning on me, as long as I focused on making sure she was safe and healthy and not facing any criticism from strangers, I could make it through this night.

19

Mia

Lucas was acting ... weird. I mean, from our little spat earlier, I knew he was nervous about meeting Lily and the gang. And the constant glares from assholes judging us definitely didn't help matters.

But this was beyond nerves.

He was being absolutely *fucking* annoying.

Once we actually got into the venue, he insisted we sit at the bar during the opener so I could get off my ankle. Then he ordered my drink and then replaced it with water barely an hour later. And then, when the concert finally got started and we elbowed our way to the stage, he kept me from dancing.

It was the third time that I started swaying to the beat and Lucas wrapped an arm around my waist, that I slapped his hand away.

"You need to cut that shit out," I hissed, stepping away to turn and face him. Lucas pulled his arm back, his eyes dropping to the floor.

"I'm just trying to make sure you don't overdo it. You're going to hurt yourself." The words were mumbled and the concert loud, but I could still hear a sort of indignation in his voice. Like he knew better than me. And that was one surefire way to piss me off.

"I'm a grown-ass woman, I know my own limits better than you. And I certainly don't need you babying me." We were starting to draw onlookers and Lucas glared in their direction, shifting on his feet.

"I'm not trying to baby you," he argued, reaching out again to grab my arm. I let him pull me closer this time but didn't nestle into him like I normally would have. Maybe it was because of all the looks we've been getting tonight, but him treating me like I was a kid rubbed me the wrong way. We hadn't really addressed the age gap, but I thought we'd gotten over it without having to have some big conversation. Were all these looks making Lucas rethink our relationship? "I just don't want you doing something you regret come the morning."

"It's a concert!" I yelled, smacking his arm off me and backing away again. His use of the word regret hit too close to home. "We're supposed to be having fun. Not making sure we're not sore in the morning."

"You don't have to be though."

"That's not for you to decide. You should trust me to make that decision for myself."

"If I can keep you from getting hurt, then I'm going to do it, Mia. Whether you're happy about it or not, your well-being comes first."

"Well then I might as well leave, huh? Since I'm not allowed to have any fun anyways." I stayed facing him long enough to watch his face drop, then turned with the intent of just getting away. Except some dude stepped in my way, a cocky smile spreading across his face.

"I can show you some fun. Way more than the old man can," the man said, eyeing my body while he licked his lips. Great, I just love random men coming onto me when I was clearly trying to leave.

"Pretty sure that *old* man can last longer in bed than you," I snarled. The man laughed it off and stepped forward, a hand moving towards my shoulder. I leaned back to dodge the touch, landing into a hard chest behind me. I didn't have to look to know it was Lucas. "Besides, pretty sure he could kick your ass too."

The guy's eyes trailed over my head to where Lucas was likely glaring at him and started backing away. He mumbled some sort of half-hearted apology to Lucas before disappearing into the crowd.

"This is why you shouldn't just wander off," Luca grumbled behind me.

What an asshole, one side of me said. *He's acting out because he's nervous and if he can deal with my baggage, I should be able to deal with his*, the other side said.

I took a deep breath and turned back to him. "Just ... give me a second, all right? I get what you're trying to do, but you're doing it in a really frustrating way. So I'm going to do the *adult thing* and take a minute to cool off."

Lucas' jaw ticked, but he nodded and walked back to where the others were standing. Both Maya and Lily looked over at me, Maya with a quirked eyebrow and Lily with a wrinkled brow. I shook my head, torn between wanting to rant about everything and not really being sure I was ready to do that with them. So instead, I went to the bathroom.

I stood in front of the sink, splashing cold water on my face as if that would calm my thoughts. But apparently, it did nothing, because when the door swung open, I jumped thinking Lucas had bragged in.

Except it wasn't Lucas. It was Maya and Lily.

"Is everything okay?" Lily asked, stepping up to my side. Maya went to my other side, setting her bag on the counter and shifting through it to touch up her makeup.

"It's fine, Lucas is just ..." I trailed off, not sure what to say. I could understand his nervousness, but I didn't have any idea what to do about it other than never take him out again.

"A controlling asshole?" Maya supplied in my silence, continuing her reputation as a take-no-shit kind of bitch. It was refreshing, especially since Carrie was still denying whatever was going on with our not-landlord.

"I mean, if that's your thing, that's totally okay," Lily said in a rush, making Maya cackle. "We're just checking in."

"Well, I won't say it isn't *my thing*," I said through a laugh. "But his sexy control thing is *way* different."

"Called it," Maya called and when I turned to her with an eyebrow raised, she sighed and put away her lip gloss. "You value sex more than a relationship. So if this man was gonna get you to call him your boyfriend, I figured he had to be good in the sack. So do you call him Daddy in bed or what?"

I rolled my eyes, smirking. It wasn't a straight answer, but Maya caught it and laughed, smacking a hand on my shoulder. On the other hand, Lily completely ignored the dirty bits and took my hand, bouncing up and down.

"I was surprised you asked to bring him! I don't think you've ever brought a guy around. That must mean he's special, right?" Lily's voice softened at the end. Lily was always soft like that. She was going to make an excellent dance teacher whenever she decided to retire from choreography.

I'd shut down that softness a lot during recovery. Even something soft irritated a fresh wound. And I was certainly guilty of snapping when I was hurt. Which probably made people stop reaching out.

And yet Lily still called me today, even after years of no talking.

"Yeah," I grumbled, guilt prompting me to open up. "He is. He's just ... not used to the looks yet. You know?"

"Aw, she's opening up. Lucas must be doing something right," Maya cooed, pinching my cheek and laughing when I smacked her hand away.

"Oh, I know. People are giving you guys such ... bad looks."

"Shitty looks, Lil. You can say shit. You're an adult and there're no kids around," Maya said before wrapping an arm around me and adding, "But if he's gonna let shit like that get to him, just dump his ass now. Men don't grow out of that shit and a lot of them get worse."

"I don't think that's true," Lily argued. "You guys haven't been together that long, right? I'm sure it'll get better."

"It has to," I said. Because if it didn't work out with Lucas, if we couldn't fix this I ... I don't know what I'd do.

"All right, I didn't mean to be a downer. How about we go back to my place and have a girls night. That'll give you guys some space for each other and maybe he'll get his head out of his ass by the morning," Maya offered. "Plus, I was really excited to see that new girl and since she's not here, I've kinda lost interest. She's so fucking hot too, she's got, like, Warped Tour, Vans everything vibes."

"Maya, you have a girlfriend!" Lily chastised.

"Oh my god, just let me be a bisexual hoe for once."

"No, you're making us look like a stereotype."

"Us?" I questioned. Because last I knew, Maya was the only bi gal in the restroom.

"Oh well, yeah ..." Lily stammered, biting her lip and looking away.

"Oh my god, it's Mia. She's not gonna out you to anyone," Maya grumbled.

"Like you just did?" Lily asked with a quirk of her eyebrow. Then she turned to me with an awkward shrug, the motion so uncharacteristically ungraceful. "I haven't told Dean yet."

"Oh shit." They'd been together since they were in *high school*. I'm pretty sure they were each others' first and only. It was a pretty big deal if she hadn't been able to tell him.

We started out the door, Maya centering herself among us with her arms over each of our shoulders. "We'll just add that to the list of things to complain about tonight. I'll make us something nice and strong –"

I stopped processing Maya's plans as my eyes adjusted to the dimness of the concert hall and I saw Lucas leaning on the wall across from the bathroom. Except he wasn't alone or with anyone else from our group. He was with a woman around his age.

And it wasn't the fact that he was talking with another woman that hit me in the gut like a fucking semi-truck. My jealous streak wasn't *that* bad.

It was the *way* he was talking to her. Relaxed, not looking over his shoulder for people staring at him or glaring other men away. He didn't have a care in the world about being around this woman and I couldn't help but think he'd be happier that way.

Lucas

Mia was right. I was keeping her from having fun because I was anxious and when I get anxious, I try to control things. And it was making her miserable.

When I told the others Mia went off, Maya and Lily exchanged a look and immediately ran off to the bathroom. If I wasn't so aggravated at myself for making this whole evening a mess, it would've warmed my heart watching the women go after my girl. Mia may have thought they weren't really close, that they'd all fallen apart, and that may have been the case with the others. But Maya and Lily still considered her a friend.

I wouldn't be surprised if they were shit-talking me in the bathroom now.

Shit.

Without a word to the others, I headed towards the bathroom and stationed myself against the wall.

I didn't know how to fix this. I'm not even sure if I could.

I loved her, there was no way I could stop worrying about her or trying to care for her.

I loved her.

I loved Mia and I was smothering her because of it.

"Lucas?" a familiar voice called, pulling me out of an impending self-loathing spiral. I looked up to see Emma, an ex-girlfriend, and her teenage boy, who made an immediate beeline to the bathroom.

The fact that I couldn't remember the kid's name was a pretty clear indicator that I was the shitty one in our relationship. We'd started dating right after my gym opened and I simply didn't care enough to spend time on our relationship when I needed to keep my business afloat. That didn't exactly make for a smooth breakup. And I'm surprised she even bothered stopping to say anything to me.

"Emma, hi, how're you?" I crossed my arms and tried to focus on the woman in front of me instead of staring at the bathroom door like a creep.

"Oh, I'm all right. Just watching over Ian, you know. Didn't really trust him and his friends on their own at this venue, especially with the older crowd. Though we're both still far older than them." She laughed, looking around the hall at the twenty-somethings that crowded the area before her gaze returned to me. "So what're you doing here?"

My fingers twitched, fighting the urge to grip my arms to alleviate the tension this question created. "I'm here with my girlfriend."

Emma's eyes widened and she looked around. Mia was probably on the older end of the fans here. Anyone older appeared to be with a kid.

"Oh," Emma started, shaking her head. "Is her kid a fan too?"

"No. She is." And then, because I felt the need to justify myself, I added, "She's 27."

"Oh," she repeated, "That's surprising."

"And why do you say that?" *Just go ahead and say it, everyone here is thinking it anyway.*

"You've always been so ... uptight. It's surprising you'd even consider dating someone so young, let alone go to a concert with them. She must be very special."

I grunt in response, not sure what else to say. It took a lot of temptation for me to ask Mia out. It took just a look to get me to this concert where I've managed to make both of us miserable. Was that a common occurrence?

Did I keep Mia from having fun all the time? What else was she missing out on because of the complications our relationship caused?

Ian stepped out of the bathroom, calling for his mom but going straight back into the crowd before she could respond. Emma rolled her eyes, murmured a goodbye, and took off. I turned my attention to the women's door and suddenly there was Mia, Maya's arm over her shoulder, the other woman chatting animatedly. Mia's eyes were on me though and she looked ... off. Like her mind was so far elsewhere, she wasn't even looking at me.

"Mia?" I stepped up to them and the other girls halted, eyes flashing between Mia and me.

"I'm leaving with Maya. I'll let you know we got there safely. Stay and have fun if you want." Mia ducked out of Maya's hold and started to the exit. I followed.

What was she thinking? Did she think Emma was hitting on me or something?

No. We might both be on the possessive side, but that sort of emotion would have elicited a stronger reaction. She would've marked me as hers, not left.

But still ... it burned *not* to explain.

"She was an ex, just saying hi. That's all, Princess." My voice was edging on pleading and I couldn't explain why. It's not like I wanted to stay at this concert. But I didn't want to be the reason she left.

Mia's steps paused at the double doors that lead to the main street and she turned to me. Her eyes were narrowed, a sharp look that wasn't hurt or angry, just ... something else.

"Well, knowing she's an ex doesn't exactly make me feel great. But I didn't think anything was going on, so no worries there. I just don't want _"

"Good," I interrupted, taking her hand. "Then let's rejoin the others. Or go to the bar so you can sit down."

Mia groaned and ripped her hand away from me. "You're not listening to me. *I'm leaving.* You can stay here or go, whatever you want. But I'm going. I can't be around you like this."

"Like what?"

"Like ... neither of us is having any fun."

We'd argued a lot over the last few months. Over petty, stupid bullshit, like how she dressed at the gym. And things that actually mattered, like what the line was for me buying her things and how involved our life would be with family. This was different. She wasn't digging her feet in or trying to get a rise out of me. She was simply done, tired. I'd done that to her.

I have to let her go.

The thought sent ice through my veins. Because I knew it was the right thing to do and the truth of it felt like dropping a weight while doing a chest press.

"Okay."

"Okay?" Mia repeated, disbelief coloring her voice. I opened my mouth to respond, but Maya rushed past me and grabbed Mia's arm. "Tell Daddy goodbye. It's time for a girls' night."

Mia looked between me and her friend and nodded.

"Night, Lucas. I'll text you later."

All I could do was nod in return and watch as Lily joined them and the girls left.

I turned back to the concert and watched. Watched people dance and drink and have fun. Watched parents shake their heads at their kids and try to corral them away from the young adults.

And I didn't fit in on either side.

So I went home and tried to come up with the words that would break my heart, but hopefully save Mia some pain in the long run.

21

Mia

"I think he's going to break up with me," I murmured to the ceiling, seven mojitos in and laying on Maya's floor.

"Me too," Lily said beside me. We were quiet for a second before she sat up, waving her hands wildly. "No, no, no. I meant Dean."

"What? No way." I tried to sit up beside her, but lightheadedness hit me with a vengeance, so I stayed on the floor.

"I dunno," Maya said, her half-full glass sloshing as she waved her hands around. "Dean has said some weird shit to me over the years. Nothing, like, crazy alarming, just some little things that make me think he's cool with the queers, but he doesn't want to *date* one."

Lily collapsed back to the floor.

"Shit, I'm sorry," I whispered, not sure what else to say. It felt like shit when Lucas just said okay to me leaving, like he saw where our relationship was starting to crumble and accepted it. But with Lily ... it wasn't even a matter of accepting it and moving on, he'd be straight up rejecting her and her identity. My issues with Lucas sounded so petty in comparison.

That had to mean something right? Like this was an issue we could fix. It didn't just boil down to incompatibility.

Or was I just not ready to let go?

"Ugh, you're both such Debbie Downers. Let's talk about something else," Maya groaned, twisting on the couch until she was upside down, head resting on the floor between Lily and me.

"You don't have to tell me, but I'm curious. How'd you figure out you were bi, Lil?" The other two looked at each other, weirdly quiet. I couldn't see their faces well, but that definitely meant something. Guess I missed out on a lot in the last few years.

"I kissed somebody and it felt … right." Lily turned the other way, facing the wall, her ears twinged pink. Then she turned back sharply, eyes wide. "I told Dean immediately! That's cheating, so of course I had to tell him. But …" Another glance to Maya, who at this point decided to sit back up, creating some distance between the two women. "He didn't think it counted as cheating because the woman … kisses a lot of people."

Oh yeah, that definitely confirmed it. They kissed. Huh. Why did I immediately want to tell Lucas and see what he thinks?

"Yeah, you should definitely dump his ass. If only because he belittled your feelings," I said and Maya, uncharacteristically just nodded in agreement.

"But I still love him," Lily whimpered, staring back at the ceiling. Maya abruptly stood and walked to the kitchen. I rested a hand on Lily, trying to be a good, supportive friend, even though the gesture felt awkward.

"I'm sorry," Lily murmured, wiping away the beginnings of tears. "We were supposed to be talking about you and Lucas. Not my problems."

"I think your ten-plus-year relationship crumbling trumps mine."

Lily shakes her head and shuffles to sit up, leaning against the couch. I follow and rest my head against her shoulder. God, I've had too much to drink. When was the last time I drank this much? Probably since before my ankle thing.

"But you love him, right?"

I groaned and Lily laughed as I pushed myself to stand. "All right, I've had enough feelings talk for now."

"That's our girl!" Maya called from the kitchen, where she'd busied herself by pouring three glasses of water. "Can we start shit-talking them now? Because I've been waiting *years* to make fun of Dean's stupid 2000s heartthrob haircut. Like, did he see one episode of Gilmore Girls and decided he wanted to truly embody that asshole?"

Lily threw her head back, laughing. "Oh my god, I told him I thought Jared Padalecki was hot in high school and he didn't talk to me for, like, a week."

"What a bitch," Maya and I murmured. And we kept going, poking fun at Lucas and Dean like we'd been friends this whole time, like there hadn't been years where I'd closed myself off. And even if I was right about Lucas wanting to give up on us, at least he helped me get to a place where I could open up to others.

22

Lucas

I hadn't been this anxious since opening the gym. But what else would I feel knowing that the best thing for Mia was letting her go?

She'd only texted me twice since the concert. Once letting me know she got to Maya's safely and would be spending the night. And then once this morning, telling me she'd swing by the gym during our lunch breaks.

It was our regular routine, but knowing today was the last day it would happen sent my heart plummeting.

I'd spent the whole night thinking about whether or not this was the right decision. But the whole time, all I could think about was the way her voice hitched when she said, "You're not listening to me." It drove me to go to the gym early and I worked through every piece of equipment with the excuse that I was doing a quality check.

She was right though. I hadn't been listening to her or paying attention to what she really needed or even wanted. She was meeting estranged friends and instead of easing her anxiety, I heightened it by adding my own. And it was just like Emma said, I was rigid and uptight. Going out wasn't my thing. Drinking on a work night wasn't my thing. And I'd do it for Mia, but I'd hit my limit eventually. I barely even lasted a night.

And it's not like the looks from others would ever ease up either. I knew our age difference was a problem, and had tried to not even look at her because of it. But when being with her felt right, I stopped caring and forgot how much of a problem it really was. Even before we got together,

I don't think I had any idea how bad the judgmental looks would be. Or how much they would get to me.

And then there was Mia's resistance to even starting a relationship in the first place. Would it be fair to push her for more, keep her while I struggled to adjust, when I was the one who asked for this in the first place? No. There wasn't room for trial and error with Mia. For all I knew each time I fucked up, she'd close off again. And then when she finally had enough or I finally couldn't handle the differences anymore, she wouldn't open up to anyone else ever again. I didn't want that for her. I wasn't even convinced she'd stick around much longer to deal with my stubborn ass self. She might like me, but she didn't love me.

It was better to stop before we hurt each other.

"Lucas?" Mia's voice drew me out of my daze and I stopped mid-way through a stroke on the rowing machine to look at her. She was dressed in dark baggy jeans and a shirt from the concert, hair half braided back, looking stunning like always. Meanwhile, I was a sweaty mess, my shirt sticking to my back and my gray hair frizzing.

I nodded towards my office and she went off without a word. I followed, slowly, trying to form the words that would break my heart.

When the door closed behind us, Mia turned to face me and I knew she knew what I was going to do. There were dark shadows under her glistening eyes and it was my fault.

"Just fucking say it already," she spat, shuffling her feet around.

"I'm sorry." The words tumbled out of my mouth before I could think better of them and Mia scoffed.

"Right, you're sorry. Me too, I guess." Her voice was laced with sarcasm but she kept her gaze on the floor, tears forming at the corners of her eyes. She was crying. I'd made her cry. I hadn't expected that. Not when she didn't want this relationship in the first place.

But the reaction did make me feel better than when I'd imagined her completely unaffected by our break up.

"It's for the best for both of us if we break up now, before ..." *Before I tell you I love you and can't let go, even when I'm making things worse.*

"Right, quit while we're ahead. Got it." She sniffled and everything shattered. I couldn't put this back together, but maybe I could get her somewhere better. Anything would be better than this.

"You didn't want this relationship in the first place, Pri – Mia." I bit my tongue, trying to hide the hurt. It might've started as a game, but I liked doting on her. Maybe she wasn't a princess in the typical sense, but she was mine. Except she wasn't anymore.

"You're right, I didn't want this. I thought that if I opened up to someone, they'd disappoint me. And then you forced me to open up and now you're proving me right." Her angry voice was so much easier to hear than her being on the edge of tears.

"But that's fine. You're just making another decision for me. I guess I should have expected that." Mia pushed past me and out the door. I should have stayed there, should have let that be the end of things. But I needed more, just a little more before I could really let go. So I followed after her, past the other gym go-ers who openly stared at us, and up to the front desk. But Mia was going to leave without looking back. So I said the only thing I could think of to get that anger directed back at me.

"I'm canceling your membership too."

Mia spun back to me, eyes bright. She stepped up to me, poking a finger at my chest.

"You think I'm so much younger than you, that I can't look after myself, but this is how you chose to break up with me? Real fucking mature, Lucas. But you know what? Two can play this game. I'll spend these last few weeks of my membership strutting around your gym in as little clothes as possible, making sure you regret this, showing you I'm worth holding on to."

And then she was gone. Storming out of the gym and unsuccessfully slamming the slow-close doors behind her. I stood there, fists tight at my side until I saw her car drive off. Then I turned away and saw Rick staring at me, wide-eyed.

"So ... do you really want me to cancel her membership, sir?"

"Of course not. Fuck," I murmured, rubbing at my eyes like I could erase everything that just happened.

23

Mia

The fact that Lucas had managed to change my habits in just a few months when my roommate couldn't even convince me to fold towels the way she liked, was telling.

And it pissed me off.

I missed waking up beside him, I missed his stupid check-in texts to see if I'd had enough water. I missed the way his skin felt under my hands, his dumb, grouchy frown. I was so mad. At him for making me fall for him and then deciding we couldn't make it. At myself for giving him that chance and letting him have so much power over my emotions. It was all so *fucking stupid*.

And I couldn't even work out my frustrations. I'd been bluffing about strutting around the gym. I didn't want to see Lucas, even thinking about the *possibility* of running into him hurt. I'd gotten so desperate to get that little dose of endorphins, that I even tried running around my apartment complex. It sucked.

So I stayed home, curled up on the couch, and rewatched Gilmore Girls. Luke reminded me of Lucas though and I might have watched the episode where he and Lorelai kissed a few times in a row.

"Oh my god, I can't take this anymore," Carrie shouted, coming into the room and snagging the remote from the coffee table to pause the show.

"Carrie, whatever this is about, I'm not in the mood." I pulled my blanket closer, poking one arm out to reach for the remote.

"Well, I'm not in the mood to deal with post-break-up wallowing any-more." Carrie held the remote behind her back and I gave up with a huff.

"How do you know about that?" I asked. I hadn't told her or even Maya and Lily about the break up yet. The more people I told, the realer it was. And if I told them, they'd ask how I was feeling and I'd have to admit I was fucking wrecked by some dumb man.

"Lucas texted me and asked that I look after you." What an asshole. "But there's not gonna be anything to look after if you rot away on the couch."

"I don't need anyone looking after me," I murmured.

"Clearly you do." She tossed the remote to the other side of the couch and plopped down beside me. "So tell me what you need. What's gonna help you feel better?"

God damn Lucas and his whole teaching me how to let others help me thing.

"I just wanna go to the gym and work out." It was one of the simpler things that would make me feel better. But that was as good a place as any to start.

"Okay, sure. Well ..." Carrie trailed off as she thought. "Are there any days Lucas doesn't work?"

Hearing his name made me cringe and I felt pathetic. "Today. He doesn't go in on Sundays. But there isn't a class on Sundays either."

"Okay, then how about those personal trainer classes?" I groaned. "I know you don't like them, but that's better than running on the treadmill, right?"

I glared at her for a moment before asking, "Are you just trying to get me out of the house so Ethan can come over?"

"No, I'm trying to help you, bitch." Carrie smacked my arm, the touch light, and walked off. I took a few seconds to debate if doing a training session was worth it. There was a chance whoever was available today would try to talk to me about Lucas. But if I were them, I would avoid that conversation like the plague, so chances are I was safe.

So, gnawing at my lip to fight the nerves, I called up the gym to make an appointment.

Lucas

I've been having a hard time staying home since Mia left.

No, she didn't leave, I told her to go.

And every goddamn place in my home reminded me of her. I heard her laugh, her cries of pleasure *everywhere*. It was like she was fucking haunting me and I deserved it. I kept checking my phone like some lovesick teenager, praying she'd call, text, or something. But I knew Mia well enough to know that she wouldn't reach out. Even if she did miss me, she'd never admit it after what I did.

So in order to keep myself sane, I worked every waking hour. I redid the financing system, took stock of all our equipment, ordered replacement items, and even took over a few dropped shifts for the front desk. And every moment was like standing on pins and needles, waiting for Mia to come in and fulfill her threat of making me regret letting her go.

"Worth holding on to." Her words replayed in my head, making every night sleepless. She was worth so much more than holding on to, she was worth letting go when I knew I was hurting her. I wish I could tell her that, make sure she understands that she's worth fucking everything in the world.

"Great form, Mia. Just four more."

Hearing her name caught me so off guard I tripped over my own feet. I turned toward the performance studio, towards the voice, and saw Mitch with Mia. They were talking, soft smiles lighting both their faces as Mia did curtsy squats. She leaned a bit too forward and Mitch leaned over, his hand going to the small of her back as he corrected her form. She looked over her shoulder, saying something that made them both laugh. I saw red.

I was miserable and she was flirting with *my fucking employee.*

Rage, jealousy, and simple volatile anger moved my feet. And before I could think better of it, I was in the room, glaring at Mitch like I wanted to murder him. I was highly considering it before Mia caught sight of me and her face dropped, that flirty smile now a mask of nothing.

"Oh hey boss, what's up?" Mitch asked when he turned to see who Mia was staring at.

"Nothing. But could you excuse us? I'd like to talk to Mia. Alone." My voice was sharper than I meant it to be, but I couldn't control it. My emotions, all for Mia, were in control now and I simultaneously loved and hated it.

"Um, is that all right with you, Mia?" Mitch asked, looking between the two of us, his body shifting slightly to come between us. If I was in the right headspace, I'd have applauded Mitch's reaction. Getting between an obviously upset man and the woman he wanted to see alone was a good thing. Checking with her was a good thing. But my body was screaming that he'd touched her and I needed to replace that touch.

Mitch was doing the right thing and I hated him for it. Hated the way Mia licked her lips like she was considering saying no.

But then Mia nodded and Mitch mumbled something about being just around the corner before leaving the room.

As soon as we were alone, I stepped into her space and kept going until she was backed up against the wall, the dip tower blocking us from view. Her eyes narrowed at me, but her chest was falling in quick waves as her body reacted to my proximity.

"What are you doing here, Lucas?" There was an angry edge to Mia's voice that cut. I wanted to kiss it away, make her melt into me.

"I could ask you the same thing. It's been over a week and I haven't seen you here once. Now all of a sudden you're in here flirting with my employees. Are you trying to make me jealous?"

"I wasn't trying to make you jealous," she huffed. "I didn't think you'd be here."

She might as well have run me over with the way those few words hurt. Because she really didn't have any reason to believe I'd be here. Sunday was normally my off day, the day we'd spend all our hours in bed.

Which meant she wasn't flirting with Mitch to get back at me or make me jealous. She was doing it just because she wanted to, because she was moving on from me.

"So you just gave up on the whole making me regret things?" I asked, my voice rough. I couldn't take this anymore. I fucking hated not having her.

"Well given how jealous you look right now, I'd say you already regret letting me go."

I huffed, bracing one arm against the wall by her head and letting my other hand trail down her arm. Goosebumps flared at my touch and I couldn't for the life of me remember how I convinced myself I would be all right without Mia.

"You're right, Princess. I'm going insane without you. I need you. *Please.*" I would beg every day for the rest of my life to get her back. But … I didn't deserve her. I'd make her miserable. I had to keep a hold of that thought, that truth.

"Well, I don't need you," she murmured, her voice weakening, that fire dulling to the warmth of lust. I reached down and grabbed her ass, hiking her up the wall and pinning her there with my hips. Mia's legs wrapped around my waist and she shook in my hold, a little whimper escaping from her lips.

"You're right, Princess. You don't need me." I grinded into her, relishing in the way she gasped. "But that doesn't mean I don't need you. So tell me not to kiss you. Tell me now and I'll go."

"You shouldn't," she whimpered, head falling to the side so I could press my lips to that delicate skin.

"That's not what I asked you."

"I thought you didn't like it when I lied, Daddy."

My teeth sunk into her neck, pressing until I knew I'd leave a mark. Then I trailed my lips up her neck, grazing her skin until I took her lips. And fuck, it had been too fucking long since I'd kissed her. It felt like I could finally breathe again. God, why did I need this girl so badly? And why couldn't I keep her without making her miserable? And why, at this moment, did I not care if I held her back as long as I could keep her?

Mia's hands tangled into my hair, pulling me closer like she was just as desperate as I was. And the noises, the *fucking noises* she made. Every breath, moan, and whimper fed me. Who was I even fucking kidding? I couldn't be without Mia. I just couldn't. I'd just have to ... fuck, I still didn't have a fix. And she deserved so much more than someone who couldn't stand going out, who couldn't handle the looks. She needed someone who was capable of not being some rigid hard-ass all the time and I –

"Fuck, Lucas, I love you."

I froze, unsure I'd heard her right over the raged sounds of our breaths.

"Fuck," Mia hissed, unraveling her legs and pushing off me. Meanwhile, I couldn't stop touching her.

What the fuck was that? She loved me? The woman who kept pushing me away, tried to make our relationship just about sex, loved me? And I gave her up.

"Mia, wait a second," I said, taking hold of her face and forcing her to meet my eyes. "You love me?"

She bit at her lips, eyes unblinking like she was trying not to cry.

"It doesn't matter."

"Of course it matters," I growled before kissing her again. Mia gasped into my mouth, moaning when our tongues met. But then she pulled back, shaking her head.

"No, it doesn't. *You* broke up with *me*. Without even telling me why. So it doesn't matter. My feelings don't matter."

"Yes, they do." God, I fucked up. "I just ... you were miserable at the concert. And everything I did, everything I am, was wrong. I'm an uptight asshole and I ..."

"Gave up." Mia's eyes went cold and she ducked out of my hold. "You couldn't control the situation like you normally do, so you gave up. So no, it doesn't matter if I love you or not, because you can't control me or the situations we'll find ourselves in with our age gap and you can't stand that."

"That's not what happened," I argued, turning to where she now stood in the middle of the room. Her face was flush, half her hair pulled out of her hair tie, and bright red splotches along her neck. It was a distracting sight. But I had to focus. "I was trying *not* to control you."

"By making a decision for me! God, Lucas. I was finally thinking I liked being in a relationship, that I'd been wrong this whole time, but then you let everything crumble because you couldn't relax for one night. And honestly, I got it. I was frustrated as fuck, but I understood why you were tense and I was willing to ... I don't know, try again later or something. But you. Gave. Up." She pointed at me with each word, poking straight into my heart. She was right. I didn't picture her even wanting to try and work through whatever bullshit my anxiety was doing. I'd never gotten past the version of Mia that didn't even want a relationship. Meanwhile, she'd grown. Fallen in love. With me.

"I thought that –"

"I don't care what you thought. You had a chance to talk to me, *like an adult*, and you chose not to." Mia turned away, scooping up her keys and bottle, before turning back to say, "Tell Mitch I'm done for the day and thanks for his time."

"I can't exactly do it like this." I gestured to my semi-hard cock, which hadn't gotten the message that Mia was done touching me. Forever.

Mia's gaze dipped to my dick and she smirked and even that look set my heart running. "That sounds like a you problem."

25

Mia

Maybe my whole post-break-up slump was just because I hadn't gotten to say my peace. And now that I had, I could accept that Lucas and I were never going to work out in a practical sense. He liked structure, I liked to do whatever the fuck I wanted. He liked to care for and control, I just wanted to be left alone. It is what it is.

Except as much as I accepted that, I still loved Lucas and missed him so damn much.

And my gym. I finally joined some stupid chain gym and the A/C never worked and they only had one Pilates class a week.

But I was fine. So fine that I'd invited Maya and Lily over to my place to do some more catching up.

"Did you hear that girl is actually touring with Homesick now and we're the only stop that missed out? I'm so pissed," Maya complained lounging across my couch like it was hers. As a good host, I didn't complain and took the floor while Lily took the remaining armchair.

"And is that the only thing you're pissed about?" I asked. Because since I'd been in an emotionally better place, I unmuted everyone from the studio on my socials and saw Annie conveniently cropped out of all the concert photos posted the next day.

"Shut up. If you make me talk about my breakup, I'll make you talk about yours." Maya tossed a pillow at me and I caught it just before it hit the TV.

"Fine, fair enough. No partner talk. Is there anything fun happening at the studio?" Both the girls let out long and disgruntled sighs before launching into a rant about how the new owner has started pushing a social media presence and forcing everyone to learn stupid TikTok dances instead of creating new routines like usual.

"I want to choreograph a routine for Bejeweled," Lily whined. Then she pushed up out of the chair and stomped over to my record collection to find the Midnights album and put it on.

"I never took you for a Swiftie," Maya commented, side-eying me. I shrugged it off, knowing all too well that if I denied it she'd quote an old argument where I may have turned the station every time Swift came on. I suppose it wasn't Taylor's fault her songs were overplayed. But there are only so many times I could hear one song in a row.

"Don't you think this would be such a fun song to choreograph, though? I'm thinking five dancers in a –" A knock at my door stopped Lily before she could undoubtedly talk us through an overly complex routine that would be outrageously stunning if it ever were to be performed.

"If it's Lucas, fuck off!" Maya yelled, not even picking up her head off the cushion.

"Um, no, it's Ethan," the man called from the other side of the door. I gave the girls a confused look, which they didn't have the context to understand, and got up to answer the door.

"Hey, Ethan. Sorry, but Carrie's not here," I said and Ethan immediately shook his head, black waves barely covering downcast green eyes.

"No, I didn't think she was. She's ... never mind. This was dropped off at the office for you." Ethan held up a purple box, brown yarn crisscrossing over it. As soon as the box was in my hands, Ethan nodded goodbye and went off. Weird. I wondered what happened between him and Carrie for him to act like that.

"Who's Ethan and why is he bringing you baked goods?" Maya asked, finally sitting up when I walked back into the room.

"Baked goods?" I repeated, looking more closely at the box and noticing a note tucked under the string, with an icon of a horizontal croissant roll and jumping cow.

"Oh, that place has the best cinnamon rolls!" Lily called from the shelves, now going through my entire collection.

"Don't change the subject." Maya threw a sharp look at Lily, but the other woman paid her no mind.

"Ethan just works at the leasing office here. It's from …" I pulled out the card and my heart jumped into my throat.

Mia,

I love you. Make sure you're taking care of yourself. And please give me another chance to take care of you again.

Lucas.

I didn't have to open the box to know it was filled with rolls. And since I couldn't stomach the thought of actually seeing the gift, I tossed it onto the coffee table and moved to the kitchen. "Help yourselves."

The girls crowded the box, quickly demolishing the food without questions. I opened up my texts with Lucas and, ignoring several apologies and promises, typed out just two words.

> **Me:** Fuck off.

It didn't take more than a minute for his reply to come through.

> **Lucas:** No. I don't make the same mistakes twice.

> **Me:** I don't either.

And then I turned off my phone. Because listening to him ask for me back hurts. If I let him back in, then what? We get to another point where he decides his control issues and anxiety are worth more than me? What was the fucking point of that?

"Hey, if Lucas is gonna beg for you back with expensive pasties, can you hold out a little longer? Those cinnamon rolls Lily loves are only served on Sundays," Maya called, waving Lucas' note over her head. I crossed the room and snatched the note away from her, crumbling it and tossing it towards the kitchen trash.

"What's your one thing?" Lily asked, her voice quiet as she looked at the now empty pastry box.

"My what?"

"That one thing he could do to wipe away your doubt." She pushed off from where she'd sat in front of the coffee table and turned back to the record shelf. "For me, it'd be Dean telling me nothing has changed. That our relationship can go on exactly the same except he can make bi-wife energy jokes and we can compare our tastes in women."

On the couch, Maya flinched. I didn't even know Dean all that well, but I couldn't picture him responding like that. And for me ...

I'm not sure what Lucas could do to make me not doubt that he'd get scared and run again. It'd have to be something big, something where he'd lose a lot more than me if he stepped away. Something that practically made it impossible for him to leave me again over something trivial. Something that made him vulnerable the way I was with him.

I shook the thoughts out of my head. There was nothing like that that he could do.

Lucas

I signed the papers this morning, praying Mia would accept them. It was the only thing I could think of to show her I could give up control. But would it be enough?

Probably not.

One gesture wouldn't be enough to prove I wouldn't get my head stuck up my ass again. But hopefully, it was enough to prove that I wouldn't run again, wouldn't talk myself into letting her go because I thought her life would be better without me, wouldn't decide that she didn't love me enough to work on my baggage. This had to show her I had more faith in our relationship than my anxiety did.

Fuck, I was anxious as hell. I needed my girl back.

Standing in front of her apartment door, I took a deep breath before knocking. Carrie, for whatever reason, was on my side. Or perhaps it was more apt to say she thought Mia was happier when we were together. So she'd confirmed Mia would be home to accept my papers. Or at least take them.

The door opened and for the briefest of seconds, I saw the love of my life standing there, shadows under her eyes and hair frizzing uncontrollably.

And then the door slammed in my face.

I bit back a growl that rose instinctively in my throat. My body reacted to her too quickly, taking the door slam as an act of brattiness that I needed to fuck out of her.

Except this wasn't bratty behavior done to get a rise out of me. This was completely justified. And I deserved worse.

"I swear to god, Lucas, if I have to get a fucking restraining order against you, you're paying for it. I don't even know if you have to pay for one, but if you don't, I'm charging $50 an hour for whatever time it takes me to file it."

My grip on the papers tightened. I knew it was unlikely she'd talk to me. I'd prepared for this.

That didn't make it any easier.

"I love you too, Mia." Another deep breath and I knelt down to slide the papers under her door. "This is ... the last thing I can offer. It's not just empty words or promises. I mean it. Every word. Just read it. Please?"

I held my breath, listening as Mia picked up the papers and started shuffling through them.

"This is a lot," she murmured. I couldn't tell if she was talking about the gesture or the amount of papers. Either way, it didn't really bode well for me.

"I don't feel like reading this now. I'll text you if I have anything to say. And that's a big if."

My breath flew out of me like someone was squeezing me from behind.

"But don't get your hopes up. I might not read it for a day or two, who knows."

Now she was being bratty. And I smiled because I missed her so damn much, even just a bit of her attitude filled me up.

"Take your time, Princess. I'll be waiting." I heard a small little huff from the other side of the door and rested my forehead against it. I wanted to see her again. That one glimpse wasn't enough, nothing would ever be enough when it came to her.

"I love you." The words slipped out, quiet and unanswered. The memory of her slipping those words out in between kisses teased me. That shouldn't have been the moment we said our first I love yous. Hopefully, I'll have the chance to make up for it.

Mia

"He gave you his gym?" Lily shouted, making half the bar turn our way.

"No way! Let me see." Maya reached out, snatching away the papers in my hands. Despite what I told Lucas, I read them as soon as I picked them up. And then I read them again and again until I was so confused I had to Google business terminology to really understand what was happening.

But it was true. Lucas signed over control of his gym to me.

I mean, not complete control. Any decisions I made had to fit the budget and it could be vetoed by an employee-selected representative and blah blah blah.

What mattered was he gave me control over the one thing he was more anxious about than me. Or maybe it was a close second, didn't matter, the gesture still stood. It was the exact kind of thing I'd thought of when Lily asked about my one thing.

"Okay, so like, you're not responsible financially if the gym goes under, right?" Maya asked, squinting at the documents.

"Nope. Gym goes under, Lucas pays for it all."

"That's so sweet," Lucy sighed, while at the same time, Maya said,

"Oh you could totally fuck him over." "Maya!" Lily yelled, slapping Maya once she'd processed what she'd said.

"What? He was a dick. And if he wants her back, he should be able to handle a little taste of his own medicine. I'm not saying make the gym go bankrupt, but like, she could paint it pink."

"I like the way you think." I grabbed Lily's bag, ignoring her outburst, and shuffled around for a pen. Finding one, I started a list on a napkin titled Gym Changes. "I'm thinking we could make it dude's only gym, with a strict no-shirt policy."

"Mia," Lily chided.

"Lil is right, I think the dude's only thing could backfire on you. Not many dudes do Pilates and you wanna keep your classes," Maya reasoned.

"True." I crossed out the dude's only line and chewed on the pen. "Definitely need more Pilates classes on the schedule. Do you think you can paint the machines without damaging them?"

"Who cares, add it to the list!"

"Don't you guys think this is a little ... childish?" Lily asked, eyes flicking between us.

I took a deep breath before admitting, "I just need to get this out of my system before I go see him."

"Aw, really?" Lily cried while Maya made a gagging face. "Okay, I'll play along then. Um, what about free hair scrunchies and pads and tampons in the women's locker room?"

"We're not listing *good ideas*," Maya said.

"Also they already do that," I added.

"Really?" Maya and Lily asked in unison.

"Right, adding Maya and Lily get in free. And on Wednesdays, you have to wear pink."

We kept going until we had a dozen unreasonable demands. Then at the bottom, I added, *Lucas has to tell Mia he loves her every other waking hour and after every orgasm.*

Three hours ago. She'd texted me three hours ago after two days of silence.

And I'd fucking wait for her all damn night, sleep under my desk if it brought her back to me just a second sooner.

Hope made me anxious for her arrival. It was already almost closing time and my office was starting to feel suffocating. But I knew Mia wouldn't have texted me if there was no chance.

So I waited. And waited, until …

"So I'm kind of your boss now, huh?"

Mia leaned against the door frame of my office, dressed in her usual leggings, faded concert tee, and flannel, even though it was getting too warm for so many layers. She smirked at me like she knew exactly what I was thinking. And god, I was desperate to kiss her.

"Yes, ma'am. You are."

"Hmm, ma'am? I like the sound of that."

"Oh really?" I stood and walked up to her, balling my hands into a fist so I wouldn't reach out and touch her. "I'll call you that whenever you like so long as you agree to all the terms."

It was the last line of the contract, but the most important. *Mia must reinstate her romantic relationship with Lucas with the condition he can make up for any mistakes within three business days.*

It might've been a stupid condition, but if I was giving her control of the second most important thing in my life, I needed in writing that she would come back to me and let me make up for my mistakes. Because I knew this would be far from the last time I fucked up.

"Oh right, your little condition at the end there." Her smile widened and my heart all but stopped. "I have a few conditions of my own too."

She pulled a napkin out of her pocket and turned it so I could read. The crumbled paper was covered in dots of condensation and barely legible pen markings, some in different handwriting. At the top was *Gym Changes* and then –

"Actually," Mia said, turning the napkin back around before tearing off the bottom. "This is the only one that matters."

She handed the scrap back to me and all that was written was, *Lucas has to tell Mia he loves her every other waking hour and after every orgasm.*

I couldn't help but laugh. I was probably grinning like an idiot, but what else could I do when I had the love of my life back?

"Is that after every orgasm of yours or mine?"

Mia licked her lips and I couldn't wait anymore. With my hands on her waist, I pulled her into the office, closing the door before pressing her against it.

When our lips met everything was right again. And it wasn't just the never-ending lust this time. It was an all-consuming love that sent every-thing abuzz. But I couldn't let myself get lost in her, not yet. I still had things I needed to say.

"I love you, Mia. So damn much. I'm sorry for ever making you feel like you weren't worth holding on to and doubting you cared enough about our relationship to deal with my anxiety. I'm sorry for deciding things without talking to you. And I'm sorry the first time we said we loved each other was like this. But I love you. And I will do better." I cupped her face, making sure those bright blue eyes met mine, and saw how serious I was, how I had dark shadows under my eyes and was on the verge of crying because I could finally hold her again. "I promise."

She was quiet for a long moment, biting at her bottom lip.

"I know I'm a good kisser, but I didn't think I was so good you'd come in your pants."

"What?" Confusion furrowed my brow as I tried to piece together what she'd just said and how it related to my apology. Her eyes lowered, a soft blush spreading over her face.

"Cause my condition was for you to tell me you love me every other hour and after every orgasm. And you said it twice there, so –"

"Princess." I hooked a finger under her chin and tilted her face up. It'd been so long since I'd seen her nervous, I almost forgot the signs.

"Yeah?"

"We haven't gotten to the orgasm part of this makeup. And unless I can *only* say I love you during those two circumstances, you're going to have to get used to hearing it a lot. Especially since I've got weeks to make up for."

"I guess I can agree to that," she mumbled. "Only if we can get to that orgasm part sooner rather than later."

I hummed, letting my hand drop to her waist as I kissed up her neck, eager to re-mark her. "Kind of inappropriate for my boss to come in while I'm working and demand orgasms."

"That's why I waited until closing."

"Oh yeah? And how long did you wait to read those papers?" I sucked at the skin under her ear and she gasped, the noise fucking delicious.

"As soon as I picked them up," she admitted.

"And when did you make up your mind?"

"Before I finished reading."

I bit her, hard. And the way she squealed and squirmed hardened me so quickly, the rush nearly left me dizzy. "So you've been keeping me waiting, Princess? You've let me spend several sleepless nights in our bed alone, miserable?"

"Do stupid shit, get stupid consequences." Her voice was breathy and I knew without touching her she was wet for me. It'd been too long since we had each other, we were wound up and needed release. But god, I wanted to punish her for making me wait so long. Especially since I knew she'd been hurting without me too.

"I love your brattiness, Mia. And I'm not going to punish you now because I just need you too fucking badly. But I'm going to come up with something real nice for you. For keeping me waiting and for flirting with Mitch."

"I wasn't –" I bit her again, then licked away the sting.

"We're not arguing right now. We're making up. Now come here."

I grabbed her by the ass and pulled her to me. She wrapped her legs around my waist and kissed my neck as I walked us to my desk. I yanked at her leggings, a seam popping before I plopped her bare ass on the cold wood. Leaving her pants and underwear around her ankles, I kissed her lips one more time before sinking down to my knees.

"I should get a pillow for the office," I murmured into her thighs, kissing up her legs as I spread them.

"Huh?" Mia already sounded dazed, her gaze softened as she looked down at me.

"Well, if my new boss is hot as fuck and in need of orgasms, my knees are gonna give out on me before I've had my fill of this pussy." I yanked her legs open further and buried my face into her. Just her smell was enough to make me drool and her taste sent me to fucking heaven. I relished in her, so relieved to have her again that I couldn't tear myself away to even look at her as she screamed my name. I'd been starving and now that I was finally being fed, I was sloppy. I sucked and licked and swirled just trying to win her orgasm as soon as possible. I needed it more than my own release.

And when she came for it was the sweetest thing I'd ever tasted. I lapped her up, slow and languid licks as her breathing went from ragged to soft. I pressed one last kiss against her cunt before standing.

"I love you, Mia. And we're definitely going to need a pillow in here for as long as I wanna go down on you." Our mouths met, tongues sliding together, and she hummed against me. All I could taste was her and I never wanted it to fade.

"Keep that up and you'll be due for a raise," she murmured against my lips.

"I don't need anything but you, princess." I knelt down again and started to pull her leggings back up.

"What?" she stumbled over the word, but still her body obeyed the unspoken command and lifted so I could get her dressed.

"I'm taking you home."

"You tired already, old man?"

"Of you?" I scooped her up by the ass and pulled her tight against my chest. "Never."

Mia

"Y ou're going to barre in a few minutes, right?"

I furrowed my brow and looked up at Lucas. He knew the gym schedule like the back of his hand and he knew my schedule even better. "Why?"

A sly grin spread across his face and my stomach did flips.

"It's time for your punishment." He waited more than two weeks to do this, I almost thought he'd decided to not punish me at all. I mean, he started it after all.

"And is the punishment that I can't go to barre?" I questioned and Lucas' grin only widened.

"No." He turned and strode back to the bedroom. It took a moment, but curiosity had me up on my feet and following. When I got to the room, he had a pair of leggings, a bra, a shirt, and ... my period panties set out on the bed.

"Um, thanks. But you know I'm not due anytime soon, right?"

"I know. But they're absorbent and you're going to need that." Lucas then held up a small box. Pictured on the front of it was a small, sort of V-shaped vibrator and a phone screen showing the app it connected to.

"Oh, no."

Impossibly, Lucas' smile grew even wider and I knew I was absolutely fucked. He pulled the box open and tossed it aside before putting the vibrator in his mouth. My cunt clenched around nothing.

"Go ahead, Princess, put it in." He held the vibrator out to me and the way my body heated should've been shameful. I mean, he is one hundred percent going to give me an orgasm in front of almost a dozen people. In his – *our gym*.

I took the toy, turning it over in my hand. It wasn't big, so surely it couldn't back much of a punch. And the part that would rub against my clit was just ribbed edges, not a sucker. Maybe this was more about edging me all class, making me desperate and needy. I could handle that.

But then the toy came to life in my hands and my soul nearly jolted out of my body.

"I won't be able to watch you the whole time, but I'll be on the bikes just outside the studio. So if you need a break or you think someone's onto us, come out for some water and give me a thumbs up." The toy died in my hands and Lucas winked. "I'll let you get ready."

Fucker.

Lucas

Mia squirmed the whole way to the gym, anticipation rubbing her nerves raw. She was so damn worked up just having the toy in, I bet she'll come as soon as I turn it on.

If I really wanted to punish her, I'd edge her the whole time. But since I couldn't exactly sit outside the studio watching the class to see when she was getting close, I decided against it. Plus I wasn't into edging, I liked making her orgasm far too much to keep her from it.

As soon as we parked, Mia was out the door, booking it into the gym before I had a chance to even unbuckle. I couldn't help but chuckle to myself as I got out. She might be giving me a disgruntled look, but she was just as excited as I was.

"Oh hey, Lucas. Mia just came in … is everything all right?" Jesse asked when I got inside. From their end, it must've looked like Mia was pissed at me.

"Yeah, we're good. Mia's just a little grumpy because I made her late."

Jesse tilted her head to the side like maybe she didn't believe the lie since there were still five minutes until class. But she shook the thought off and focused on a customer that came in behind me. I waved goodbye and headed for the studio. Mia had already put her shoes in the cubby and gone inside, sitting on a mat, distinctly not looking in my direction.

I settled down on the benches across from the studio and slowly shuffled through my bag, changing shoes, taking out my water bottle, anything to make my delay here look natural. Several times, I caught Mia's eyes flashing away from me. She fiddled with the hem of her shirt, her phone, nervous energy bouncing off of her. It was adorable. I couldn't wait to see her squirm more, to see the mess she'd make.

Class started and Mia took a deep breath before standing and going through the warm-ups. The music was just loud enough that it would cover the sound of the vibrator. I pulled up the app and turned the toy on for just a moment, smirking when Mia flinched. She kept her eyes on the instructor, biting her lip as I tested the settings, gauging how far I could push her without risking getting caught. And when I got to the second highest pulse setting, Mia's eyes flashed to mine through the window, her pupils wide and face flushed. That's my girl.

Satisfied seeing her first orgasm, I moved over to a bike to start my own workout. I let Mia rest for a few minutes, but when the music drifting from the studio thumped louder, I pulled my phone back out and fired it up. I tapped the button in time with the music, short buzzes that were likely driving her insane. And while the thought of her squirming hardened me, one song's length was more than enough teasing.

I kept the toy on, slowly increasing the intensity so that she had just enough time to get used to the vibrations before they changed. And just as I was about to press it up to the highest level, I heard the click of the studio door and turned to see Mia walking to the water coolers. Her face was set in a scowl, glaring at me with more irritation than I'd ever seen. She was sweatier than I'd seen too, drops of perspiration rolling down the side of her face. Her ponytail was a mess, steps slow. If anyone else looked at her, they'd think she was in the middle of a tough workout. But I could see the strain in her eyes, the way her pupils flared.

I increased the toy's speed and Mia jerked, her eyes flashing to mine. I held my breath, waiting for her to give me the symbol to stop. Instead, she poured herself some water and closed her eyes as she down the cup.

Finished, she threw the plastic cup in the trash and flicked me off before going back into the studio.

God, I fucking love this woman.

31

Mia

My legs were normally pretty wobbly after barre. But after barre and constant vibrations up my cunt, I could barely even wobble out of the door.

It wasn't the buzzing that killed me, it was the way Lucas toyed with the levels, up and down, up and down. I'm pretty sure my tongue was bleeding in multiple spots from where I bit down to muffle a gasp or moan.

"How many?" Lucas asked once I finally sat down on the benches outside the studio, a cocky grin lighting his face. He hadn't even turned the damn toy off yet, just left it on a low buzz that made me want to rock my hips forward and grind my swollen clit against it.

"Four," I grumbled. Focusing on emptying my cubby instead of Lucas' growing ego.

"Good." He took my hand, pulling me up before I could get my shoes. "We've got the sauna booked."

And off he went, dragging me behind and through the doors that led to the sauna. The front room split into two changing rooms, with the already steam-filled sauna door at the back. Lucas let go of my hand to lock the front door then picked me up and carried me straight into the sauna.

"I'm pretty sure you're supposed to rinse off before you go in here," I murmured as I kissed the sharp stubble along his jaw. Now that I was alone, the irritation of having been toyed with was gone and all I was left with was the need to have him.

"But then I wouldn't be able to see the results." Lucas sat on the wooden bench and stood me up between his legs. In one quick motion, he gripped the waistband of my bottom layers and yanked them down to my knees. He pulled at my underwear, stretching so he could examine the mess I'd made. He dragged one finger through my come and brought it to his mouth, closing his eyes as he moaned from my taste. "You came so much, Princess."

"Lucas, can I just get on your cock now?" I whined, unable to wait any longer. Lucas chuckled but pushed my pants further down so I could step out of everything. With that done, Lucas nudged my stance wider, palming the toy, and grinding it into me. "Lucas."

"Hmm, it wouldn't be much of a punishment if I gave you what you wanted right away." Slowly, tortuously slowly, he pulled the vibrator out. Carefully, he held the toy in the curve of his hand so that my come didn't touch my skin when he pulled me close.

"Tell me, Princess," he murmured, pulling my shirt up with one hand to the top of my cleavage. The other hand moved the vibrator to my ass, the tip pushing just enough to make me tense. "Have you ever done anything back here?"

I gripped his shoulders, my body tilting forward as my legs gave up on me. Burying my face into his neck, I shook my head. The toy pushed against my ass, the sting making my cunt pulse.

"Fuck," Lucas hissed, tossing the toy on the bench before pulling his shorts down just enough to release his cock. I didn't waste any time climbing on top of him and impaling myself. I was so fucking wet, he slid right in, perfectly filling me in a way the toy couldn't.

"Fuck, Mia. Do you like the idea of me taking one of your firsts as much as I do?" Lucas groaned and I responded by grinding into him, using his pelvis to stimulate my clit.

"You going to take the rest of my first, huh?"

"Absa–" *thrust* "–fucking–" *thrut* "–lutely," *thrust*. Lucas pounded up into me and it was all I could do to hold onto him. My limbs were jelly, my mind blank, the only thing I could think of was the building pleasure that was about to crash through me.

"My first husband too?"

Lucas' movements stopped and that's when I really processed what slipped out in a haze of pre-orgasm bliss. Fuck.

I shouldn't have said that. Not now, not after we'd just gotten back together. And certainly not when we hadn't even known each other for a year. God damn it, the man made me feel safe expressing my emotions and now every single thing was coming out unfiltered.

I pushed one foot up to get off him, but Lucas' hands dug into my waist and held me in place. His hand snaked up my back, pressing me into him and tangling his fingers in my hair.

"Have you been thinking about marriage, Princess?" Lucas pulled my hair tight so I was forced to look him in the eye. His cock twitched inside me when our eyes met, finding the answer before I could form it into words. "I need to hear you say it."

"Yeah, I guess." I tried to shuffle, my mind racing in a very different way than my body. But Lucas wasn't letting me go anywhere. The bastard was going to make me talk about my feelings again, while his cock was buried inside me. "I'm not *that* young. Lots of people my age are married already, so I've thought about it. And with you … it's just nice. When I think about it, it feels right."

Lucas' lips crashed to mine and suddenly he was consuming me with so much passion I couldn't distinguish where I ended and he began.

"I'm not just going to be your first husband, I'll be your only one," he growled, his kisses trailing down my cheeks to my jaw to the spot just below my ear that he liked to mark. And even though I knew it was coming, when his teeth dug into my skin, everything tensed. "I don't care what odds I have to beat, I'm seeing you until the end of your days."

"Lucas, it was just –" Words were so damn hard when he was fucking me to oblivion and his words made me want to cry from just how goddamn much I loved him and how I knew, without a shadow of a doubt, that he meant every word he said.

"I don't care if it was a slip of the tongue. Consider yourself engaged. We'll go pick you out a ring tomorrow. So tell me, who's cock are you about to come all over?"

Too much, it was all too much for me to process. Too much love for him and the future he was promising me. And god fucking damn it, this had to be the wildest proposal ever.

"Daddy's cock."

The smack of Lucas' hand on my ass was so loud, I wouldn't be surprised if everyone in the gym heard it.

"We're not playing that game right now. *Who's cock are you on? Who's going to make you come?*"

"My fiancé." The words came out in a whimper as Lucas slammed me down and started moving my hips so I'd grind into him. The burn of my orgasm spread so fast, I barely had a chance to breathe between tremors.

"That's right, Princess. Come all over your husband. I'm right behind you. Always will be. Til death do us part."

K.E. Monteith is an anxious hot mess that writes about people like her fall in love and get spicy. You'll usually find her talking about her dogs, complaining about chronic pain, or screaming about something DropOut related or her current hyper fixation.

Sign up for her newsletter for bonus scenes, giveaways, and more.

www.ingramcontent.com/pod-product-compliance
Lightning Source LLC
Chambersburg PA
CBHW070821170726
48000CB00019B/1870